The welcome wagon

The bell rings before I have a chance to write back. Not that I would have had any idea what to say, anyway, seeing as how I've clearly been struck by sudden-onset escaped-mental-patient brain. I'm stuffing my books into my messenger bag, thinking about how he's probably congratulating himself on dodging a close one and reconsidering the whole welcome-wagon thing, when all at once he's back. He's *back*. Face-boy appears, all smiling and chirpy like a cartoon character, looming over me.

"Sorry about that," he says, before I can come up with an opening line of my own.

Sorry? What's he sorry about? I'm the one who was incapable of basic human interaction.

"Um, what?" *Oh, Aggie. Do go on. Dazzle him with your razor-sharp wit and keen conversational skills, why don't you?*

"The note. I shouldn't have risked getting you in trouble on your first day, but I'm kind of dying to get the scoop on your father."

So I was right: it *was* him who sent me the note. Nice. My integration into the Traynor student body hasn't gone completely unnoticed, after all.

But. This guy is interested in hearing about my family. My wack-a-doodle insane, you-can't-even-imagine, crazy-pants-to-the-*maximus* family.

As Mom might say: *Ay, Dios mío.*

Other Books You May Enjoy

Cindy Ella   Robin Palmer

Enthusiasm   Polly Shulman

Falling in Love with English Boys   Melissa Jensen

Geek Charming   Robin Palmer

Geek Magnet   Kieran Scott

I Was a Non-Blonde Cheerleader   Kieran Scott

My Most Excellent Year   Steve Kluger

When It Happens   Susane Colasanti

S.A.S.S.: Up Over Down Under   Micol Ostow & Noah Harlan

S.A.S.S.: Westminster Abby   Micol Ostow

WHAT WOULD MY CELL PHONE DO?

by

Micol Ostow

speak

An Imprint of Penguin Group (USA) Inc.

YPF
Ostow

Published by the Penguin Group
Penguin Group (USA) Inc., 345 Hudson Street, New York, New York 10014, U.S.A.
Penguin Group (Canada), 90 Eglinton Avenue East, Suite 700,
Toronto, Ontario, Canada M4P 2Y3 (a division of Pearson Penguin Canada Inc.)
Penguin Books Ltd, 80 Strand, London WC2R 0RL, England
Penguin Ireland, 25 St Stephen's Green, Dublin 2, Ireland (a division of Penguin Books Ltd)
Penguin Group (Australia), 250 Camberwell Road, Camberwell, Victoria 3124, Australia
(a division of Pearson Australia Group Pty Ltd)
Penguin Books India Pvt Ltd, 11 Community Centre,
Panchsheel Park, New Delhi - 110 017, India
Penguin Group (NZ), 67 Apollo Drive, Rosedale,
Auckland 0632, New Zealand
(a division of Pearson New Zealand Ltd.)
Penguin Books (South Africa) (Pty) Ltd, 24 Sturdee Avenue,
Rosebank, Johannesburg 2196, South Africa

Registered Offices: Penguin Books Ltd, 80 Strand, London WC2R 0RL, England

First published in the United States of America by Speak, an imprint of Penguin Group (USA) Inc., 2011

1 3 5 7 9 10 8 6 4 2

LIBRARY OF CONGRESS CATALOGING-IN-PUBLICATION DATA IS AVAILABLE

Speak ISBN 978-0-14-241469-9

For the VCFA Revisionistas:
Kate Angelella (always an honorary),
Lynda Graham-Barber, Gwenda Bond,
Gene Brenek, Galen Longstreth, and
Shawn Stout. Long live Betsy's!

Fact: Every March, Anchorage, Alaska, is host to the prestigious Iditarod Trail Sled Dog Race, which kicks off ceremoniously on downtown Fourth Avenue. The Iditarod is the longest and most famous sled dog race in the world.

Question: Famous compared to *what*?

I'd like to tell you that my parents

haven't always been certifiably, 161 percent, *mucho*-major-mondo bonkers.

I'd like to tell you that, but it would be a big, fat lie.

So if we're going to be all truthful and stuff, here it is:

Truthfully, it's kind of weird having a celebrity shrink for a father. More so if said father can't seem to get through a single conversation, *ever,* without referencing Oedipal complexes, oral fixation, or compulsive behavior.

Like, a Reese's Peanut Butter Cup addiction is *so* not "compulsive behavior."

Am I right, or am I right, people?

(And for the record, I *never* wanted to marry my father. Because: gross.)

Mom is no better; she's a retired telenovela star with zero concept of the word *understated.* Everything about my mother is colorful and loud, just like our sprawling, psychedelic penthouse back in Miami (thank you, gurus of the Estrellita! network, for the constant, reliable, and oh-so-*generoso* stream of residuals). Loud and colorful = just the way Mom likes it.

Which is why I completely can't believe that she's gone along with Dad's questionable flash of inspiration that has us trekking way the ell-hay up to Denville, Alaska. To live.

(Twenty miles northwest of Anchorage; population 16,093, if you were curious. Though, I guess that'll technically be 96, once we, the Eckharts, are all settled in.)

Now. I don't really know all that much about Alaska; in fact, most of my assumptions about the place I've picked up from old Chilly Willy cartoons or recent Presidential debates. And to be honest, I'm not so sure that either resource is big with the factual accuracy. Is Chilly Willy even *from* Alaska, come to think of it? He might be firmly Antarctic-based, and this whole line of thinking, in addition to being a twelve out of ten on the absurdity scale, is a big, sloppy mental detour.

Make that a thirteen out of ten. When you're looking to an animated penguin for answers, it's safe to say you've officially bottomed out. Willy, dude, you let me down.

Still. Within the population of our little three-person family unit, I can assure you that I am the least pathetic of us all (not that I'm biased or anything). I'm not my dad, chasing after a pipe dream of becoming an Inuit Dr. Phil (reach for the stars!). And I'm most definitely not my mamacita, who, upon hearing about this proposed Arctic expedition, clapped her palms together and announced with a flourish what a sheer and utter relief (*"mira! estaba muy cansada!"*) it would be to take some very welcome time off from her extremely demanding job of spritzing her J-Lo–esque locks with enough Aqua Net to qualify her as a one-woman eco-hazard and shrieking memorized, melodramatic lines in a foreign language on film—the minute that my father suggested it.

(The move, that is. Suggested the move.)

Nope. They're them, and I'm me. Agatha Eckhart, conscientious objector. I am totally anti this tundra transplant. And while I may not be colorful like my mother, I can be quietly, powerfully forceful. Or so I'd like to think. I've been kicking and screaming the whole way toward the North Pole.

"*Aggie. Dios mío.* Can you please. Stop. Kicking. My seat."

See? Kicking.

Technically, I had to take a pass on the screaming—the FAA frowns on that sort of behavior—but I've made up for it by kicking at the back of my mother's seat accidentally-on-purpose for the last thirty minutes. Dad would call this "textbook passive-aggressive behavior." If he were paying any attention to me at all, that is. I'm stealthy, though.

Really, it's less of a sharp punt and more of a steady jiggle; if I wanted to, I could chalk it up to nerves. Which is what I do.

"Sorry, Mom. I guess I'm just anxious."

Anxious. Ha! Anxious would be a gloriously welcome change of pace. Anxious would be a *relief*, bar none. Right now I am eons beyond anxious. I'm so freaked out that there is currently a conga line of teeny tiny caterpillars step-kicking through my stomach. And for the record, the caterpillars are freaked out, too.

"*Sí, m'hijita.* It's because of the turbulence. But I don't think Ricky Ricardo appreciates your contribution to his in-flight experience."

Ah, yes. Ricky Ricardo. Perhaps the one thing in my mother's life that is *not* larger than life, Ricky Ricardo is her Chihuahua. He is a mousy fawn color and eensy enough to fit in the palm of my hand, trembling and blinking and generally resembling nothing so much as a slightly overgrown rat.

Chihuahuas, like my borderline-oversized butt, are proof positive that nature has a sense of humor. As near as I can tell, Ricky Ricardo serves no discernible purpose save to provide my mother with the delicate plaything that I could never be. She loves him more than just about anything else in her life, self included (no joke).

See, whereas my mother's Cuban curves can best be described as va-va-voom, my own DNA instead wove itself together into some sort of cruel practical joke. As a result, I'm stuck in a kind of quasi-cherubic limbo, soft and rounded in most places, kinda like an overgrown toddler (sex-ay). Unlike Ricky Ricardo, who is dainty and fragile (that trembling! that blinking!), and therefore the one, of the two of us, who can generally be found sporting a matching ensemble to whatever fashion atrocity Mom has committed to for the afternoon. Right now, for example, he is decked out in a Chew-cy Couture velour hoodie bedazzled with his own initials: RRE (for Ricky Ricardo Eckhart, obvs), to coordinate with Mom's official flying uniform, a sunset-orange tracksuit.

Pity the little rodent can't read. That custom monogram is wasted on him.

"Sorry," I mumble. Ricky Ricardo may be my number one rival for my mother's affection, but I don't really need to contribute to his misery. Right now, I know from misery. I wouldn't want to add to another living creature's experience of it. He's the closest thing I have to a sibling, after all, and we're going to have to band together in this time of need. Or something.

I wait a beat to see if my father is going to weigh in on this conversation. But through the space between his and my mother's seats, I can see that he has his earphones plugged in and is blissfully oblivious to the Eckhart Women's Celebrity Non-Death Match, round infinity. I know that he's deep into the latest "Mental Health and You!" podcast, or something like that. Surveying the competition and whatever. Those things are like crack to him. Right now I could probably parachute from the emergency exit—using Ricky Ricardo as my parachute, monogrammed hoodie and all—and he wouldn't blink. Dad's headphones are noise-canceling, too. He ordered them special from a scary-fancy European Web site and everything.

"De nada. Never mind," Mom says briskly, waving her right arm in a swooping arc, causing a clatter as the translucent bangles on her wrist knock together. "Ricky forgives you. He told me."

He told her. He *told* her. Um. Crazy-pants.

"But you know, Aggie," she goes on, "you'd probably be less anxious if you weren't eating so much candy, *sí?* The sugar goes straight to your bloodstream. Don't go filling up on junk food. It's not good for you."

Right.

Fact: chocolate is the number one *proven* mood enhancer. Seriously! I read it in *Cosmo* once. And while Dad is more than happy to pass out prescriptions to the masses like he's the pharmaceutical version of Walmart, apparently he holds his own flesh and blood to an entirely different level of chemical independence.

Pfft.

As you can see, chocolate is my only recourse.

"I don't have any junk food," I say, sullen.

It's true; I don't. Not anymore, anyway. I scarfed down a clandestine bag of peanut M&M's before boarding, back when we were delayed at the gate, my back turned outward so I'd be hidden from Mom as I practically gobbled them whole, like aspirin or Ritalin. When it comes to my own method of self-medicating, the woman simply does not see things my way. To her, I am not only huge. I am a huge disappointment as well.

For the record, I am a size 10. Would I rather be a size 6? Sure. I mean, who wouldn't? Then I could, like, share clothes with D list actresses on random CW television shows. But I guess I want chocolate more than I want to be a size 6, because when it comes down to a battle between peanut M&M's and my willpower, my willpower loses. Every single time.

So when I reach my leg out again and resume jiggling, prompting a muffled squeal from Ricky Ricardo, I decide to chalk it up to a chronic lack of inner strength.

I should work on that, I guess.

CHAPTER 2

It could be worse.

At least I'm not depressed.

Then again, if I were depressed, my father would possibly know how to handle me.

My father is Robert "Dr. Bob" Eckhart, a "depression specialist" and high-profile psychiatrist and psycho-pharmacologist who has cracked the treatment of clinical depression wide open. Seriously, he's like the pied piper of Miami neurotics. Of which—who knew?—it turns out there are quite a few.

Of course, it being South Florida and all, the Miami neurotics are exceptionally flamboyant, larger-than-life, and colorful, even in their gray, moody tendencies. I don't mean to sound insensitive, but it's hard to feel too sorry for a desperate hausfrau scowling through her weekly mani-pedi.

(Who scowls through a pedicure? Who can be so aggressively agitated during a heated foot massage? Really, who?)

Still, these are the women who have built my father's career. In the past ten years, he's gone from a licensed clinician working out of a low-rent strip-mall office space, to a local celebrity running a perky weekly "Dear Dr. Abby" sort of column in the paper and online.

> *Dear Dr. Eckhart: My husband is too tied up in his job.*
> Set up date nights once a week where the two of you really *focus* on each other.

> *Dear Dr. Eckhart: I think my toddler has ADHD.*
> You know, X, there are some wonderful medications available these days.

> *Dear Dr. Eckhart: My mother is a former Senorita del Mundo Latino, and she is way obsessed with my appearance. I think I have a retaliatory reverse eating disorder kind of thing going on (does that even exist?)— but I'm not down with the extra padding on my butt! Talk about cutting off your nose to spite your fanny . . .*
> *So, what now?*

Never mind, scratch that last one. Obviously, the question is my own, and I already know that my father doesn't have a response at the ready. This answer is evasive, oblique, and seductive, lurking quietly, menacingly, at the scraped-wax bottom of a pint of Häagen-Dazs Chocolate Chocolate Chip.

Which may or may not go a ways toward explaining why my mother is constantly shooting a laser-sharp beam of scrutiny straight into my soft, chewy core.

.ıll

My best friend Chloe was, in her own words, "mega-psyched" about this trip. Ever since Dad made his national debut on a certain mainstream television personality's (hint: rhymes with "soap-rah") program, he's been somewhat of a celebrity himself. Chloe almost passed out from excitement when she heard that he was being given his very own satellite radio show through which to chronicle his efforts at treating seasonal affective disorder among the Alaskan population. Apparently it's dark all the time there in the winter, and everyone is twelve kinds of bummed about it.

As someone who finds the relentless heat of the Sunshine State equally oppressive, I have to say: I think the all-powerful "theys" in charge of this disaster *might* just be barking up the wrong tree in assuming that Dr. Bob is their great white hope.

But Chloe? Chloe keeps trying to convince me that going

to Alaska will be exciting. Exhilarating. An adventure.

Have I mentioned I hate adventure?

Call me a party pooper, but the fact remains that I have no interest in adventure. I am 460 percent adventure-averse. I like me a good, solid routine. Being Chloe's sidekick—keeping secrets and keeping her boys-in-waiting entertained while she primps, preens, and weighs their respective pros and cons? That works for me. That, and my favorite purple drawstring skirt.

Unfortunately, I had to leave the skirt in Florida. Not much use for it out here, if Wikipedia is to be trusted.

(Layering: one possible positive aspect to this whole northern expedition. I like me some layers. Mmm, comfy.)

"The station sent a nice car, *sí?*" Mom observes as we pull smoothly out of the short-term parking lot of the airport and head east toward Anchorage.

Sí, senora. They certainly did. They sent a big, anti-environment, gas-guzzling SUV for us in honor of our arrival. This is our car for as long as we're up here poking around the North Pole. It's a pukey shade of pea green, and it confuses me temporarily. I thought Alaskans were outdoorsy, unsmoggy, all pro-nature and stuff. Then again, winters here are, like, *Winters.* With a capital "W," you know? (See above re: *layering*.) So I guess in this case, practicality tops politics.

"They want to keep us happy," my father booms, a drop more heartily than could be considered natural. He reaches out, places his hand over my mother's knee, and gives a reassuring squeeze. "We're big fish."

"In a skating pond, *querido*. Is not as *fabulosa* as a swimming pool, you know."

I can't see Mom's face from my perch in the backseat, but somehow, I can still hear her doubt loud and clear. For all of her enthusiasm about taking some time off from acting, she's definitely wary about making the transition from Latina beauty princess to full-on Ice Queen. Marisol Ramon-Jorges (yeah, that's her stage name) doesn't do long johns. And she might go into vitamin D deficiency if she can't lay out on Saturday afternoons.

"Wait until you see the house," my father continues, either downright oblivious or deliberately choosing to ignore the waver in her voice (or possibly even a little bit of both). "It's beautiful."

He's actually talking mostly to me. The two of them have seen pictures online, but I am a holdout, a silent but stubborn protester. I refused to look, refused to have anything to do with this migration project, until the penultimate moment possible. I packed only under *extreme* duress. I didn't have much by way of igloo-ready separates; what *does* one pack when expecting to be blizzard-bound, anyway?

"It's *rustic*," my mother chimes in, rolling her *r* with gusto. From his perch on her lap, swathed now in a neon-yellow parka, Ricky Ricardo sneezes in agreement.

I'm glad she's so pleased about it. To me, "rustic" sounds more like "septic," or "low carb." Rustic could be Really Bad News.

(Side note: this whole low-carb phenom is really one big conspiracy theory, yes?)

"It's a change of pace, that's for sure!" my father says cheerfully, whistling as though things are deliriously perfect and we're all just as thrilled to be here—in this car, in the suburbs, in *Alaska*—as he is. Maybe he's been hitting the happy pills himself lately.

He could totally do that. Pop some Xanax surreptitiously and call it research. I mean, that's his job. Snapping people out of their little internal ruts. That's why we're here, now, after all.

If you don't know (which, maybe you don't. I mean, *I* didn't, until a few months ago when it all became relevant to my so-called life), depression has hit an all-time high in Alaska, especially during the winter season. Suicides have spiked and divorces have doubled, despite the fact that the man-to-woman ratio here is something like 3:1. People are grayer and moodier than they used to be—*much* grayer and moodier than anyone I ever knew in Miami, even the cranky trophy wives who hang at the local nail salons (frankly, in Miami, *I* was the grayest, moodiest person I knew).

The sun goes down for, like, *ever* here, come November, and the days are only a few hours long. Also, it's cold. *Very* cold. Like, hypothermia cold. Meanwhile, up until last week, the only outerwear I even owned was a fleece-lined denim jacket from Old Navy that, while adorable, would be woefully insufficient up here on my own little personal ice floe.

Maybe I should have been kinder to, or more tolerant of, all of those bored, soulless women in the spa back home. From what I understand, spa manicures are difficult to come by in Denville, Alaska.

It doesn't matter (to them, not to me. Pedicures will always matter to me. While I'm not the kind of girl who normally goes in for major pampering, I maintain that pedicures are the great equalizer; no matter what dress size a girl wears, her toes look pretty and clean after a good pedi. That is a scientific fact. And nobody gives you any cankle grief when you're paying them to fancify your feet).

I don't know the cankle count of the population of Denville, but as I say, it kind of doesn't matter. Soon, all those mopey Denvillians won't need superficial treatments like seaweed wraps and silk tips anyway. Soon, my father will have worked his magic-psycho-mojo on them all, will have restored tranquillity to Alaska's winter of discontent.

He was hired in the grand tradition of show business; his column had become a sort of pop-culture phenomenon back in Miami, and then spread like wildfire over the Internet. Meanwhile, the Alaskan Chamber of Commerce decided that something had to be done about the collective bum out and everybody being so blah-blah hand-wringy and shivery all the time.

The solution was obvious (I mean, not to me, but to Alaska, I guess): bring in a flashy, accessible hotshot known for experimenting with cutting-edge treatments. My father would hold regular office hours Monday through Thursday, throwing pills at people right and left and generally giving the old prescription pad a good workout.

And on Friday, he was on the air. Syndicated through the fifty states.

My dad, the celebrity shrink. In *Alaska*, with my *mamacita* and me.

It's insane. *Totalmente loco.* Crazy enough that I have to wonder if we aren't all having one massive, collective hallucination.

Dad's been aggressively chipper about the whole thing. (Can you blame him? This is his sixteenth minute, and counting.) Mom, on the other hand, tries to play it Polly Positive, but is *obvs* torn. While she loved the idea that Dad was going to be a big star, she clearly had reservations about thermal underwear. She's not used to having to conceal her midriff.

You can see the conflict.

I didn't bother to point out that he isn't *really* a star; I mean, it's not like he's ever going to dip his handprints into the Hollywood Walk of Fame, or donate his leather-bound *DSM IV* library to the Hard Rock Cafe. I doubt that he'd even have any success selling off his medical diploma on eBay. But I had about as much say in the matter as an ice cube, and the truth is, there's at least one pro to the move, when it comes to my lifestyle.

See, I myself am kind of okay about thermal underwear. Like I said, I'm not in any great rush to shed six thousand pounds, but believe it or not, size 10 is pretty much considered plus-sized in Florida, the land of string bikinis and spray-on tans. So the idea of thermal underwear—and the layers that generally go on top of it—works for big old me.

I miss Chloe already, yes, and I miss flip-flops, iced lattes, and even the humidity, a little bit. There was something about being a sidekick, you know? Something safe and comfortable, like a wash-worn purple cotton drawstring skirt. With Chloe I never had to be anything other than the mostly quiet, occasionally funny, but always, *always* touting the status quo, best-gal *chica* girlfriend that I am.

But I guess, sometimes, you just have to compromise.

Who knows? This could be a fresh start for me. I could take on winter sports, Get Fit, Tone Up in Time for Summer!, as *Allure* advises at least once a month. Everything could change for me here.

Or? I could curl up in front of a fireplace and hibernate until springtime.

Yeah. The second option. That one works for me.

I rub my fist against the car window to clear up some of the fog that's accumulated. Outside, the landscape is vast and glittery. The glare from the snow is blinding as an eclipse, and the trees are a vibrant, lush green. It is the exact opposite of Miami, in every possible way. But at least my anti-UV sunglasses will come in handy.

In the front of the car, my mother breathes in sharply. "*Caramba!* So many things to photograph. *Mira* —just look at all of this . . . *nature*! All of this white. It is like a blank slate. Empty. *Perfecto*. Remind me, Roberto, that my camera is in the pink Louis Vuitton hatbox."

"But you . . . ," I trail off. *Clearly haven't forgotten.* There's no way she'd "forget" about her latest obsession (*speaking* of "compulsive behaviors," by the by . . .). Once it was all fully confirmed and finalized that we were northbound, Mom decided that this was her opportunity to *finalmente* nurture her big artistic passion: photography. She's decided that after lo so many years on the opposite side of the lens, she has an "innate eye for composition." Personally, I'm not so sure it works that way.

Anyway. She doesn't reply to my almost-comment. She's too busy taking in all of the *emptiness,* the blankness that stretches out before us.

I want to tell her that white is not the absence of color, but rather, the negative shade formed when all the colors on the spectrum are joined together. What's whizzing along outside of our car windows is exactly the opposite of nothing, of blankness. It's all, total, everything, and I'm a little bit sad for her that she can't see as much for herself as I can.

In the end, though, I sigh, shake my head, and lean back in my seat. I'm silent, as usual. Black, not white.

Of the two of us, she's the one maintaining the sunny outlook. Who am I to judge, then? So I don't say anything.

What would be the point?

CHAPTER 3

"Aggie. *Espérate*. Hold still while I zip this."

My afternoon bonding session with Mom has taken a turn for the horrifying.

It's not completely her fault, I know. The thing is that "downtown" Denville is really just a diner, a library, and an army-navy surplus store. I mean, I think there might be some other shops and restaurants or whatever down the various side streets, but it isn't like we're going to accidentally stumble onto the secret, undercover, hidden Rodeo Drive of the Arctic Circle.

Anyway, you know how some girls play with Barbie? Like, they'll have the dream house, and the pink convertible car, and an entire closet full of clothes for this weirdly proportioned, creepy little doll? Well, I'd bet my contraband stash of Sweet Tarts that my mother was big into Barbie when she was little. Or the Cuban equivalent thereof.

Now, I'm her Barbie. And after fifteen years of playing

dress-up, I have learned that my proportions are equally as frightening as Barbie's gravity-defying mega-measurements, but for entirely different reasons. And my mom's an angry six-year-old stabbing at my synthetic hair with a dull set of safety scissors.

I am a colossal disappointment. Emphasis on the word *colossal*.

I was the trial daughter, I think. A test run, or something. My mother always seems to be preoccupied, ever vigilantly on the lookout for her unborn supermodel-to-be. Unfortunately, after I was born the doctor told my parents, *"Nada más."* Complications during delivery and other scary, multisyllabic medical terms. Suffice it to say, other issues aside, I don't think Moms was thrilled to learn that I was both the beginning and the end of the dream.

It makes me crazy. I mean, it's *ten pounds*. At most. Ten pounds, and a reluctance to wear anything more than a spritz of anti-frizz spray in my honestly-not-all-that-frizzy hair. So I'm not a super-maxi-ultra-in-your-face girlie-girl type. So shades of gray tend to feel safer. So *sometimes* I hide size-L bod behind my skinny-minnie best friend's plus-sized personality.

So *what*?

I'll tell you what: even when I'm feeling kind of okay about being more Kelly Clarkson than Nicole Richie,

Mom's around to remind me that my own version of "almost" is never quite enough. That even the lowest of D-list celebrities—you know, the ones even *Star* magazine thinks are lame—yeah, even they have master airbrush artists tracking their every daily, publicity-driven move.

I have no such airbrushers. I *had* Chloe, my biggest champion, happy to let me play Betty to her Veronica. But now? No best friend, and certainly no one to run mom interference re: my less-than-waifish frame. Which Mom herself, currently struggling to fasten what is perhaps less of a jacket and more of a flotation device around my torso, tersely reminds me.

"*Dios mío,*" she breathes, finally gaining purchase with the zipper. "This coat is a size large."

Shocked. I am shocked. A size *large*? *Moi*? Never. *Dios mío,* indeed!

"It's a junior." I ball my fists up tightly at my sides to avoid breaking into an animalistic scream and fleeing from the store, half-fastened, purloined parka clinging fiercely to my supersized body and all. From inside my mother's quilted Chanel carrying case, Ricky Ricardo shoots me a sympathetic look.

As if the dude could possibly hope to understand my trauma.

Everyone knows that junior sizes run small. I read it in

Seventeen. It's a conspiracy against those of us who are doubly cursed with both butts *and* boobs. Puberty: truly, a natural disaster.

My mother is not impressed. She snaps the jacket shut imperiously so that I am tightly encased. None of my extra poundage will escape from this jacket. The world has been spared the sight of my full frame for one more day.

"*M'hija*," she reminds me, "you *are* a junior."

.ııl

Cute coats are only for skinny girls, anyway. Girls like Chloe, or even my mother, who, while technically a woman, is built more like a genetically gifted high school student. Girls who garner a second glance when doing nothing more glamorous than walking down the street. I have long since resigned myself to the knowledge that I am too repulsive to deserve to squash my big ole bod into anything other than a nylon life raft. There's a reason Mom starves herself into an entirely different shape than the one that the Good Lord of Caloric Distribution saw fit to give us both, a reason that she wears her hair long and blond rather than settling for the somewhere-between-dirty-blond-and-actual-full-on-brunette shade that came with the genetic package.

It's the same reason I had banished myself to the store's

back corner in the first place, where a wide and varied collection of girth-appropriate puffy coats hung in wait. It was a struggle to talk Mom out of the pink-and-lime-green houndstooth-checked peacoat, but well worth the effort.

Eventually, she finds a size large that is generously cut, and boxy. I talk her out of the proposed candy-apple-red version—red being Mom's signature color, but not so much for me—and back to basic black. After enough whining, she caves. How could she not? The truth about my body, my shape, my . . . *me* is self evident; anywhere I turn, all I can see are my own rounded hips and full face reflected back at me. This store was obviously built from one giant omni-mirror, designed by a person who clearly hates curves, and I mean, you just can't argue with the truth. Especially not when you've got reliable visual aids on hand.

So, the black parka it is. Size *large*.

Like me.

.ıl

Sitting shotgun in the SUV on our way home from the store, the enormous parka tamed into submission and stuffed into the back, I can't help but play Chloe to my own psyche. She may not be here, but I know what her take would be. She'd want me to go with the red jacket. *No, thanks.* I reassure myself that the black jacket will be just fine. It probably won't get as dirty as the red one would have, either, or if it does, the dirt won't show. Dirt doesn't show as much on black, right? Also, black is way more slimming than red, at least according to *Elle*—another bonus for the Coat That Ate Alaska.

I've almost managed to convince the Chloe-me. Almost.

I reach for the radio knobs and turn the dial to my favorite station out of habit. Static screeches through the atmosphere, causing my mother to clench the steering wheel tightly. Her knuckles drain of color, and the veins on the back of her hands throb.

"Sorry." Of course, we're way out of range for Miami stations. Or, for that matter, anything else transmitting from the U.S. mainland. I mean, we're practically living on a glacier, for Pete's sake. I hit Seek and watch the numbers fly off in opposite directions until they come to agree on a random frequency and, of their own accord, settle again. The latest in pop-punk-blond, bland ridiculousness shrieks at us desperately. The speakers in this car are high quality and thus capture every trip up the electronic scale. I think my ears are going to bleed, but whatever.

Mom's over it, though, totally not listening anymore, to me or to the radio.

Her hands have relaxed, flesh-toned and healthy-looking

again, and she's not doing the upsetting mouth-breathing thing. Even Ricky Ricardo seems more chill, snoring away lightly in my lap like a miniature heating pad.

"Aggie, *mira*." Mom waves her repinked right hand in the general direction of the monstrous dashboard. "I think that's your school."

Sure enough, we zip right past a sort of run-down, but still pretty imperious-looking brick building. The stone carving over the front doorway reads TRAYNOR PUBLIC HIGH SCHOOL.

Traynor's classes started in early September, so I've missed only about a month of school. It took longer than we expected for Dad to finalize his satellite radio deal, but once that was all sewn up, the rest of the relocation plans fell into place pretty swiftly. At least I won't be too far behind everyone else. The principal wrote a long e-mail to me (well, really to my parents) explaining as much. He is looking forward to meeting me, he said, and he is sure the other students will be welcoming and helpful. He is *sure*.

The thought doesn't do nearly as much as I'd hoped to quiet the hummingbirds playing racquetball against my rib cage. I mean, what a waste. Starting all over again from the social equivalent of square one, I mean. Back in Florida, I'd worked damn hard to get myself knighted the Best Friend.

The Best Friend doesn't have to wear halter tops, or

do the limbo at sweet-sixteen parties. She doesn't have to straight-iron her hair if it's raining outside; everyone pretty much *expects* the Best Friend's ponytail to curl up slightly at the tips in inclement weather. And let me tell you: it takes the pressure off. The Best Friend really has only two jobs: to be friends with the prom queen, and to be funny. Which I was. But not without effort. I worked for it, busted my (considerable) butt to secure my place in the pecking order. And for what?

Who knows if I'll be able to reclaim that comfortable nonspace, that nontitle, that power nonposition here in Denville? Maybe Denville has a different social hierarchy. Maybe here, it's bad to be green-eyed, or to wear red Converse low-tops without the laces (people here probably mostly wear snow boots, right?). Maybe people in Denville think therapy is weird and, by extension, will assume that my family and I are crazy (which, between you and me, may be true, but I was kind of hoping to keep a lid on that info for at least a few days).

I just have no idea.

That's the real *pro about the black puffy parka,* I realize, blinking. *The anonymity.*

In a black puffy parka, I could be any other student: a jock; a math nerd; a sensitive, artsy type. Chloe and the Best Friend need not exist in black-puffy-parka-land.

Or—and this is the really appealing alternative—if I wanted, I could be invisible. I could be no one.

No one at all.

.ıl

As it turns out, a high percentage of our breakables have arrived in Alaska . . . broken, including Ricky Ricardo's engraved Riedel crystal drinking bowl. This unfortunate reality pushes my mother to the brink of a housewares-induced breakdown. It's tragicomic, really; this place may be a high-falutin', recently developed McMansion (seriously, this house is, like, the complete opposite of *rustic*), but the bulk of its inhabitants, both human and inanimate, have been shattered to smithereens.

For his part, Ricky Ricardo seems entirely unconcerned as he slurps water from a small plastic Tupperware container that we managed to fish out of the wreckage. His makeshift dish is set against the picture window that runs the length of our living room wall, but I doubt he's appreciating the view.

Mom clenches her jaw, which may or may not be an improvement compared to the mouth breathing. From my perch at the adjacent coffee table, I lean as far forward into my *OK* magazine as I physically can, smudging newsprint across the tip of my nose in the process.

"Ugh. Go wash your face, Aggie."

She's not even looking at me! She is hunched over a smallish, sealed box on the living room floor, sliding it back and forth with an ear cocked to the ground. The box's contents rattle ominously. She is all-knowing. But how? Disturbing. I rub my nose self-consciously.

"I said *wash* it, Aggie, not poke at it. You're just going to make that gunk harder to scrub off. *Por favor.*"

Fair enough. But still: it's *my* nose, not hers. Maybe I wanted it gunky.

"We should all get showered. Clean up."

Dad's chipper voice breaks the icy silence with forced cheer. He is fast running out of Ways to Cajole My Mother. I can hear it in his voice; his falsetto rivals the latest boy-band confection. "Wash the day off. It's been a long one."

He's right, and he's also wrong.

He's right because we arrived yesterday straight from the airport, and collapsed, clutching lone, loose sheets and throw pillows, directly onto our unmade beds. Dad offered to take care of the unpacking this morning (he's still trhying to get in good with Mom after the whole broken-breakables thing), thus freeing Mom up to drive me into town and attempt to dress me up like permafrost Barbie. Time spent shopping with my mother tends to pass as slowly as dog years, or, more appropriatcly, as continental drift.

So yeah, it's been a really long day, and I wouldn't mind taking a dirty-nosedive back onto my hastily assembled bed upstairs.

He's wrong, though, because although we're still in the early stages of fall, Alaska is already welcoming the advent of near-constant evening, making the actual day quite short. It was pitch-black when we found the house last night, and our eyes played tricks on us as we squinted to decipher street signs. A small town, with fewer high-rises, means ink-black skylines, as well. It was like feeling our way through a photo negative.

Through our picture window, we have a prime view when the sun begins to roll downward, toward the earth. Right now, sunset starts at six-thirty P.M., but before we know it, we'll be watching the sky streak pink and orange blazes starting around four. I kind of can't decide how I feel about that.

I mean, there's got to be a reason that bears hibernate through the winter, right?

Did I say, "Soon enough"?

Um. Not quite.

Alas, first, there is dinner. Dad hustles us into the bathroom one at a time so that we can each run a brush through our hair and rinse the stubborn moving grime out from underneath our fingernails (I also have to remove the imprint of *OK* magazine from my face, of course, but that gives way quickly under a splash of warm water). He's taking us out, in theory because he wants to "experience Denville!" (implied enthusiastic punctuation his), but probably more because he doesn't want to call any further attention to Mom's demolished collection of Tiffany champagne flutes.

So. The dining situation in Denville. It's sort of . . . well, it's sort of nonexistent. Except for one bare-bones pizza parlor, a Mexican fast-food joint, and the diner that Mom and I found when we were shopping, that is. The radio station people promised Dad that Alaska takes a turn toward the cosmopolitan the closer you get to Anchorage proper, but for tonight, we're slumming it. Mom has made it perfectly clear that she's done enough exploring for today as it is. The sunny mask she's been sporting since we left Florida is slipping. Dad's pleas to leave Ricky Ricardo at home for the night probably didn't help matters much, either, his argument being that there was no telling whether Denville eateries are canine-friendly. This is the type of town where people keep sled dogs, I think. And not as pets so much as workers. I'm not sure they'd even see Ricky Ricardo as a dog rather than a species unto himself. Dad's point was a valid one, but obviously Mom didn't see it that way.

Or maybe she's just overdue for a microdermabrasion session or something. Which might be hard to come by here in Denville.

"This is cozy, isn't it?" Dad waggles his eyebrows at me over the gargantuan plastic-coated diner menu that's open in his lap.

It must be said: my father is a good guy, for the most part, but I am sorry to tell you that when he waggles his eyebrows, he looks like a Muppet. This makes it somewhat difficult to take him too seriously. Besides, his tone is way too lighthearted for the current circumstances, anyhow. Methinks Mom's chimichangas are about to burn if we don't get some service here, *pronto*.

But anyway—sure, okay. I don't have major issues with the old-school decor here, all vinyl, linoleum, and chipped plastic. Still, "cozy" might be kind of a stretch. It's chilly in here in the same way that it's been chilly ever since we stepped off of the airplane; there's a creeping shiver here that crawls along the surface of your skin and burrows deep into your bones. The bite in the air here makes me grateful for the extra padding on my hips and thighs, for my self-created layer of insulation.

I used to think that Miami weather was the worst; the constant, cloying, cotton-wool humidity and the unrelenting sun. The way the rain would burst through without warning, pelting against windows, sidewalks, windshields. The fact that people coped by wearing white short shorts and candy-colored tank tops with straps as thin as dental floss, while I suffered silently, swathed in kinda-trendy/mostly shapeless cotton sundresses and flip-flops.

I thought the switch to northern climes would be trading up; jeans and sweaters are sort of the great human equalizers, you know? But it's not a trade up. It's a total trade-*off*. A damp chill has latched onto my skin with tiny, stubborn little claws, the way your shadow does at twilight.

Which is particularly funny, seeing as how, soon enough, twilight will be starting around lunchtime here. What is that? How do people here deal?

Oh, right: that's where Dad comes in.

"So," my father tries again, cautiously. He fiddles with his silverware, then pushes it away, toward the middle of the table. "Have you spoken to Chloe? I'll bet you have lots to tell her about this place."

Uh, no. If I were going to contact Chloe, it would be strictly to transmit some Internet version of a Morse code SOS: *Save Our Sidekick.*

I'm reluctant to share the details of my personal trauma with Chloe. The Best Friend's primary role is to maintain a placid, upbeat demeanor, after all. Also, she might not exactly be able to relate. She is the most popular girl in our junior class, if not the whole high school. She has hair the color of polished onyx, and eyes that are either blue or green, depending on what she's wearing. She is extremely disciplined about her daily regimen of power yoga, Neutrogena Build-a-Tan, and Crest Whitestrips, and it totally pays off. She is also in honors English and she serves as Student Council treasurer. Are you nauseous yet? She would be very easy to hate, if only she weren't so freaking nice. Like truly, genuinely *nice.*

Bitch.

People sometimes wonder how someone like me got to be such good friends with someone like Chloe. We met in kindergarten. There's just something about bonding over who gets dibs on the berry cherry glitter marker that apparently ties you for life.

(Yeah, I let her use it first. But you guessed that already, right?)

According to Chloe herself, I'm "hysterical" and "a good listener" (and—oh!—I have "a really pretty face," too). And see, that's the thing about being a little bit bigger, a little bit of a wallflower—you're not a threat to anyone, so as long as you practice good personal hygiene, and brush up on your conversational skills, you're in. So it's not like I'm some kind of freakazoid pariah, despite what you might be thinking. Sure, I may stick to the sidelines, but in Miami, at least, I had the social scene figured out.

But anyway, no. I haven't spoken to her yet. The Internet isn't up yet at our place, I remind my father.

"What about your cell phone?"

He nods toward my place setting, as though expecting the phone to be resting daintily on my bread plate or something. Which it is not. I mean, *rudeness*, please. If there's one thing I can't stand, it's people blabbing away on cell phones in public places like restaurants and waiting rooms and stuff. Mom and Dad are both addicted to theirs, so you can sort of see how it would become a pet peeve of mine.

My new phone is FANCY, with a capital "fance," and scripted in calligraphy with a flourish at the tip of the "y." It does about sixty-four zillion things that electronic devices were never meant to do, and it could probably even tell your fortune for you, if you asked it nicely. It's brand new. I haven't even taken the plastic film off of the screen yet. Dad bought it for me the day that he and Mom told me we were moving to Alaska. He's not above bribery, that Dr. Bob.

The phone is really cool, with about a thousand and one bonus functions that I can't figure out—I think you can even make microwave popcorn with it, for serious—but unfortunately, there's no one for me to reach out and touch right now. Chloe is queen; I'm her lady-in-waiting. I'm the girl with all of the "personality." I don't want to call her and whine about how you need, like, night-vision goggles to drive to brunch here at the North Pole.

My father is distracted by the waitress, a middle-aged woman with tight, wiry hair that wants to be auburn but has taken a wild left turn with something closer to Cheeto. She's ready to take our orders, but I briefly take a mini-vacation inside my brain. I am completely out of it, staring off into nowhere, when the front door to the diner opens, setting off a little bell that's rigged to ring whenever someone comes inside. Very clever system, that.

More interesting than the bell, though, is the boy who caused it to ring.

The entire atmosphere of the room alters as he steps through the door. The skin on my face and my forearms feels prickly and hot, no joke—he is *that* cute. Since he isn't looking anywhere in my direction, I allow myself a good, long ogle.

He's tall, but not, you know, freakishly so, and slight, but not so skinny that a hug from me would crush his spine. So that's a check in the "positive" column. I'm not exactly sure where the idea of hugging him came from, but it makes the prickly heat flare to the very tips of my ears, almost like an allergic reaction, if allergies were at all sexy or romantic. The effect is not altogether unpleasant, so I decide just to let myself go with it.

His hair is light brown, and rumpled. His boots are forest-green, and hard-core. He's wearing a wool peacoat—it's black, like my parka, which clearly means that we are meant to be together for all eternity, or at least maybe for this semester.

Swoon.

"*Agacita*." My mother taps me on the shoulder with a sharp, manicured fingertip.

"Huh?" Oh, right. Dinner. I haven't even glanced at the menu. "I'll have . . . um . . . a hamburger."

My mother coughs into her fist. Subtle. She believes that red meat gives you cellulite. I think she saw that on *The*

Tyra Show once. How she would know from cellulite is beyond me. To the best of my knowledge, she's never had so much as a ripple of cottage cheese anywhere on her body. And honestly, I doubt she's ingested any red meat since the late seventies, if family lore is to be believed.

"A turkey burger," I quickly amend. My peacoated soul mate has settled himself in at the counter. He rubs his hands together, shaking the brisk outside air off. He does not notice, has not noticed me. It's that invisibility cloak again, a by-product of the whole Best Friend, Lady-in-Waiting phenomenon.

Mom drums her pointy fingernails against the scratched, worn tabletop, silent. They are mauve today, and flawless, despite all of the scrabbling with packing tape and boxes. I know this silence, this aggressive mode of stealth communication. Know it well. Not even a *Dios mío*, which means that I am testing her patience, to be sure. The myth of the turkey burger is an Atkins conspiracy. Kelly Ripa told her so.

I bite my lip. "A veggie burger. Please." Even though the mere suggestion of soy makes my stomach flip inside out.

(Plants masquerading as meat? *Pass*.)

Whatever. I'll eat the veggie burger. I'll deal. It could be that my peacoated soul mate is a vegetarian. This could be my in with him. Maybe he'll catch my eye across the crowded diner, wink at me, and we'll run off to start our own fully sustainable, eco-conscious vegan soy plantation right here in this very town. And live happily ever after, even without meat.

I mean, you just never know.

As it turns out, Bored Mom

is about thirty-eight times more dangerous than Busy Mom. Busy Mom may have lots of "constructive criticism" for me, which is, er . . . irritating (to put it delicately). But Bored Mom? Bored Mom, it seems, is desperately seeking her muse.

It's so not going to be me.

I wake on Sunday morning to the mechanical click of a digital camera. When I blink my eyes open, I see that Ricky Ricardo has been positioned precariously against the curve of my stomach (I'm prone to sleeping curled up in the fetal position. I'm sure my dad would have plenty to say about that, but hey—I'm not about to ask him).

For his part, Ricky looks as confused as I feel.

"So cute!" Mom shrieks, nodding. It's unclear whether she means me, or the dog, or the unlikely combination of the two of us nestled together. "But it's time to get up."

I groan. "School starts tomorrow. Can't I have one day to sleep in?"

Yeah, no. Resistance is futile. "Aggie, we have to go shopping! *Vámanos!*"

Now I prop myself up on my elbows, still bleary and no less confused. "But we went shopping yesterday." My boring new puffy parka is testament to that fact. Or was that just a fever dream brought on by a close encounter with hypothermia?

She sighs as though it is thoroughly unfathomable how completely clueless I am. Which: maybe so, but I'd still rather sleep in. She says, "Yes, I know this. That was for your *chaqueta*. But we need to buy you an outfit for school."

Ricky Ricardo doesn't know what to say to this, and neither do I.

"I have pictures," she goes on, stepping forward and waving torn pages from a magazine toward me. "Is from *Us Weekly*—'Stars Bundle Up for Fall'!"

A bad feeling comes over me. I reach to snatch the magazine pages out of her hand, but she jumps back. She's spry, my mom. "Two words," she says, smiling knowingly. "Skinny *cheans*. And *h'*Uggs."

Oh, lordy. Uggs. She means Uggs.

"Mom," I say, biting back the sigh that rises in my throat. "That's three words."

"*Sí, sí.*" She waves her hand, the magazine pages fanning

the air in front of my face and making Ricky Ricardo's ears twitch. "Is no matter." She is steadfast. "Get dressed."

Bored Mom hath spoken.

.ıll

The first day of a new high school is without a doubt a particularly insidious form of torture. There should be laws to prevent it and stuff. Seriously.

Generally speaking, I'm pretty okay about school itself. I mean, I'm not a brainiac or anything, but I do well in most of my classes.

(So, yeah—I guess *maybe* it's a cheat that back in ninth grade when we first had to pick our electives, I chose Spanish as my foreign language, but whatever. Don't judge; sometimes a girl just has to go for the easy A, right? Besides, textbook Spanish is totally different than my mother's hybrid Cuban English pidgin speak, and I could—and did—argue that all I wanted was to get in touch with my Latina roots.)

But I digress. Where was I?

Ah, yes: School. First Day. Torture.

Awesome.

At Traynor, the lockers are painted a muddy shade of tapioca-beige, whereas at my old school, they were more of a vomit-green. But that's the biggest difference that I've seen so far. Beyond that, things here seem pretty status quo. I managed to talk Mom out of accompanying me to the school counselor's office this morning for my orientation, but just barely. Of course, there was a price to be paid, in the form of the newly purchased long sweater/skinny jeans/ boots combo she's squeezed me into for my Traynor Public dazzling debut.

Long sweaters and skinny jeans *tucked into boots*: the sartorial equivalent of a highlighting pen for your hips.

Why?

"*Sí*, Agatha, *es perfecto*," Mom insisted. "Practical, but trendy! You look adorable."

"You sound like an infomercial."

I contemplated my reflection in the full-length mirror of the master bathroom. Adorable, I was not. Girls like Chloe are adorable. Girls like me? We're passable. We'll do in a pinch.

Passable and *adorable* are two very different adjectives.

But at least the tunic was a charcoal gray as opposed to something downright terrifying, like horizontal watermelon stripes, or neon paisley, or whatever. Maybe Mom does understand me the eensiest bit, after all.

Um. Right.

Still, in situations like these, it's important to look on the bright side. It's not as if I'd had any great epiphanies of my own as to how to dress for my first day of school, anyway. If left to my own devices, I probably would have rocked some jeans and a hoodie, maybe some Chucks if I was feeling extra expressive; I haven't even really unpacked anything other than my pajamas and a few pairs of track pants. And I *definitely* wasn't going to call or e-mail Chloe to ask for advice. October in Miami usually means a denim jacket over your sundress, so she's not exactly prepped for my current crisis. And freaking out about how to dress for snowdrift school is pathetic, especially when your best friend is back home driving around in her convertible Beemer with the *top down*, like some kind of ad for vitamin D.

Hmmph.

Harsh reality: obsessing about my former life isn't going to change the fact that I've actually been dropped smack-dab into this one. As much as I wish it could. Actually, a snowdrift would be pretty welcome right about now.

I glance at the printed card in my hand, a welcome present from Laura Drucker, LSW, Student Counselor Extraordinaire. It's my schedule, with my homeroom stamped on it in stark black type like a Go to Jail card from a Monopoly game.

Do not *pass Go. Do* not *collect $200.*

Have I mentioned I hate board games?

Room 306. That's the number on the card, and—funny how these things work—the number on the window of the door that stands before me. Has been standing before me for the past six minutes and twenty-seven seconds. Not that I've been counting.

The only thing worse than walking into a classroom where everyone's already been seated, and you don't even know a single solitary soul, has got to be walking into a classroom where everyone's already been seated, and you don't even know a single solitary soul, *and you're wearing skinny jeans even though you're not especially skinny.*

Gawd help me.

But that divine-intervention snowdrift thing isn't happening, and I know I can't put this off any longer. I take a deep breath, step forward, and, with my right hand, I open the door to my homeroom.

My left hand is thrust into the pocket of my sweater, though. And secretly, I've got my (bare, understated, nails-bitten-to-the-quick) fingers crossed.

..ıl

The note hits my left shoulder and bounces onto the surface of my desk.

It's a balled-up wad of paper that is pinched so tightly, at first I think it's someone's gum wrapper, until I realize that it's lined, like a notepad, rather than shiny, like foil. Definitely a note. For *me.*

Highly preferable to being pelted with wayward trash. But curious: I haven't even met anyone yet, and imaginary-type friends are usually not so much with the written communication.

I hazard a furtive glance toward Mr. Markman, he of the unfortunate comb-over and master of my homeroom. Markman is distracted, deeply engaged in outlining on the blackboard the major outcomes of Roosevelt's New Deal.

We covered this already, last year, at my school in Florida. Score one for an overlap in interstate curriculum; now I know I can coast through at least one of my courses this semester. When he welcomed me to the class, Markman took pains to mention, in a depressingly earnest tone, that he was available for any after-school tutelage I might need in order to catch up.

I'm sure he was just being nice, but still: blergh.

Extra classes. No, thank you.

At least he didn't make me stand up in front of the classroom and do a whole "getting to know you" thing. That would have been unbearable, ratcheted up a notch to unspeakable if you factor in the skinny-jeans situation (they're tight and kinda constricting, despite the fact that the label insists they're constructed of "67 percent spandex"). Instead, he just waved me through the front door, briefly asserting to the rows of unimpressed faces, "I know you'll all do everything you can to help Agatha feel at home here at Traynor."

I coughed and tugged at the hem of my sweater. "Aggie." My voice sounded foreign and scratchy, like an ancient, warped record played backward, and at the wrong speed. "Um, that's what I go by—Aggie."

If it had looked as though any of the kids in the class were paying attention to me, I would have been mortified. But thankfully, no one seemed even to register the fact that a new girl had walked into the room.

Mom would be so disappointed to learn that her styling efforts hadn't warranted a second glance. That, or I would have gotten a smug "I told you so" regarding my stubborn refusal to wear heels with my *ensemble*.

"Hmm? Oh, yes. Aggie." Markman beamed, flashing coffee-stained teeth, as I ducked into one of the only remaining open seats, mercifully tucked in the far corner of the classroom.

(I'm not so big on "participation," you know? Tucked away in a back row is where it's at, where I belong.)

So here I am now, Wallflower syndrome in full effect, secreted away where I thought I'd be safe from . . . well, everything. But it's *a* back row, not *the* back row, meaning that there are still some students chilling out behind me, enjoying a nice, short-range scope-out of the back of my neck. And even all curled up into myself like a snail's shell, evidently, there is someone—a not-imaginary someone, yet—sitting right behind me, somewhere in that back row, who has seen fit to make first contact.

Hence, the note. Still sitting in plain sight on my desk.

I frown, reach forward, and uncrumple it, scanning quickly.

Is it true your father is Oprah's personal shrink?

No. No, it is not, as a matter of fact. Sadly.

But the query gets me thinking again, wondering about what people have heard, if anything, about me, and about my family. One person, at least, is interested in what the unholy heck we're doing here, and obviously knows a little something about our sitch.

But is that a good thing or a bad thing?

And just who, exactly, is my newfound stalker anyway?

I shift in my seat as casually as I can and tilt to the right, scanning the room. Mostly, I see guys and girls in various stages of acute boredom: eyes glazed over, mouths open slightly, chins slumped heavily in cupped palms.

(Side note: Markman's really going to have to step it up if he wants to rouse the zombie patrol here.)

I hear an almost-imperceptible tapping sound at my right, and when I twist again, I see that it's the sound of a pencil being drummed against a desk. I follow the pencil (mechanical, if you're curious, but otherwise unremarkable) up the length of a flannel-clad arm. A boy-arm, to be precise.

The arm is attached, as so many arms are, to a torso, and above that, there is a face. A *cute* face.

Specifically, a wide, open face dotted with a smattering of freckles just dusting the nose, and clear blue eyes like you'd see on a commercial for colored contact lenses. This face is playful, inquisitive, and it seems only logical that it would be capped off by a shaggy mop of loose, sandy brown curls that are casually tousled, but somehow not sloppy. (Whenever *I* aim for "tousled," I end up somewhere closer to the vicinity of "escaped mental patient.")

All in all, it's a pretty good face.

Just as I'm thinking that it's the sort of face to put a girl at ease, the corners of it crinkle up and one eye closes in a sly wink.

Agh. Face-boy. Is winking *at me*. He has caught me ogling and is now surely wondering what is up with my obsessive staring thing. He probably thinks I'm special needs. Although, what would I be doing in his homeroom, then?

Enough, Aggie. At a loss, I give Face-boy a halfhearted grin that should do nothing to reassure him of my emotional stability, and spin back around in my seat, mortified.

But it doesn't quiet the rusted, squeaky gears that clank and turn inside my brain. Just why *was* he winking, anyway? Winking suggests that he doesn't mind my near-clinical levels of social awkwardness. That he wasn't irreversibly repulsed by the slight bulge in my waistband where my love handles squish together when I sit, even though he has a primo view of said bulging. Winking suggests that he was just waiting for me to turn around and shoot him a look . . . that he was *expecting* it . . .

. . . that he was the one who wrote me the note.

Oh.

The bell rings before I have a chance to write back. Not that I would have had any idea what to say, anyway, seeing as how I've clearly been struck by sudden-onset escaped-mental-patient brain. I'm stuffing my books into my messenger bag, thinking about how he's probably congratulating himself on dodging a close one and reconsidering the whole welcome-wagon thing, when all at once he's back. He's *back*. Face-boy appears, all smiling and chirpy like a cartoon character, looming over me.

"Sorry about that," he says, before I can come up with an opening line of my own.

Sorry? What's he sorry about? I'm the one who was incapable of basic human interaction.

"Um, what?" *Oh, Aggie. Do go on. Dazzle him with your razor-sharp wit and keen conversational skills, why don't you?*

"The note. I shouldn't have risked getting you in trouble

on your first day, but I'm kind of dying to get the scoop on your father."

So I was right: it *was* him who sent me the note. Nice. My integration into the Traynor student body hasn't gone completely unnoticed, after all.

But. This guy is interested in hearing about my family. My wack-a-doodle insane, you-can't-even-imagine, crazy-pants-to-the-*maximus* family.

As Mom might say: *Ay, Dios mío.*

Someone smoother, more confident than me, would be able to parlay this interest in my family's . . . uh, *quirks* into some kind of mystique. Social currency. Not me. I'm just tongue-tied and frozen like a deer in headlights. Whose hooves are also glued to the road with industrial-strength adhesive.

"I'm Duncan," Face-boy says, holding out a hand for me to shake. Obviously, he's mistaken my silence for hesitance, which I kind of don't mind, seeing as how it's preferable to the truth: I'm suffering from some kind of random cognitive misfire, or a comprehensive chemical imbalance.

"Aggie," I manage, even though he probably already knows that.

"I know who you are, *Aggie*," he says, grinning and confirming my suspicions. "*Everyone* does. We don't get too many new students here at Traynor. I should know—I was the last one. And that was back in kindergarten. Anyway, your dad's radio show is big news around Denville."

"Right."

"So is it true that he's best friends with Oprah?"

This kid so clearly wants that to be the truth that it crushes me to have to say no and dash his dreams of celebrity-by-proxy. Especially since I'm sure his interest level in me will decline exponentially the minute he hears that I'm not exactly close, personal buddies with anyone you'd read about in *In Touch*.

But still. Beauty is truth and truth beauty, and stuff. Or something.

"Sorry." I think for a moment. "He's done some part-nering with Jillian Michaels, though. Like, visiting those people who are so fat they can't get out of bed? He has, uh, special drug therapies to boost their metabolism."

Ah, the morbidly obese—always a fun topic of discussion among cute high school boy-types. *Aggie, you are so on today, it's unbelievable. You've totally and completely closed this deal,* chica.

It occurs to me that bringing up weight issues is an especially bad idea at this precise moment in time, given that I'm presently zipped so tightly into a bolt of premium stretch denim that I just know I'll have zipper tracks on my pelvis for days. Gah. If only a meteor would come crashing through the building and crush me where I stand, *right now . . .*

I pause, waiting for it. Almost expecting it. Like it would almost make sense if the universe collapsed into itself right here and now and saved me from my own antisocial tendencies.

But. Amazingly, though no meteor comes careening through the atmosphere to rescue me, something almost as wild happens: Duncan laughs. A real laugh, not the uneasy, clearly-this-chick-is off-her-meds high-pitched giggle that the moment actually calls for.

I like this guy.

"That's pretty awesome," he says, laughter dying down to a few unself-conscious snorts.

He *snorts.* Okay, I *love* this guy.

"What do you have next?"

I glance at my schedule. "Lit?" I don't know why I say it as though it's a question. "Lit."

"Cool. I've got bio, but your classroom is on the way. I can walk you."

"Cool."

And it is. Cool, I mean. *Mucho* with the cool, as my mother would say.

Could it be that I've actually made my first friend here, already?

Score one for the skinny jeans—and for Mom, however grudgingly—then.

Du...

with...
dri...
me that he is...
only on what he's seen s...
Maybe *he's* the one with the chem...
means I've got someone other than Ricky Ric...
in, potentially, I'm all for it.

(Ricky's a pretty good listener, mostly, but he's lacking in the advice department, I must say. It's a language barrier thing, what with his not speaking English, and, also, you know, *being a dog*, and all.)

Traynor is a smallish school, but it turns out, when every single student is pouring out of the building at the exact same time, the overall effect is kinda overwhelming. Watching grinning faces that seem to have jumped, fully formed, straight out of an energy drink commercial spill past me makes me feel officially overwhelmed. It's nothing

like the chaos of Ocean D...
obviously—back home, it's...
fruit color schemes every...
a tidal wave of teena...
even if they are bu...
shades of mud.
I stand bac...
Wish flee...
I didn...
today...
eve...

ive back in South Beach,

tanned, bare skin and juicy-

where you look—but still. It's like

ers coming at me. It's intimidating,

dled up in jeans and fleeces in various

and let them wash over me. Soak it all in.

tingly that I'd brought my umbrella.

get any weird looks or comments about my outfit

—that I noticed, anyway—but looking around at

yone, it's easy to see that in Denville, function trumps

ashion. Nobody here is emulating the fashion spreads seen in *Us Weekly*, and that's not necessarily a bad thing. Hiking boots stomp eagerly, tipped by the hems of frayed, decidedly nonpremium denim. Tops are mostly sweaters and coats like you might find in a mail-order catalog, worn without any neo-prepster irony, that I can see.

A chirping sound shrieks from my own pocket—Ricky Martin, "She Bangs." Mom. I grab at my phone, relieved that everyone's so busy not seeing me that they also don't hear my own homage to the Latin-pop explosion of the new millennium.

I mean—"She Bangs." Cheesy. Embarrassing. And yet, oddly perfect for Mom. I flip the phone open. "Hey."

"*Agacita!* How was the first day of the *e*-school? Did

everyone like your *cheans*?" She sounds breathless, which means she was either slogging it out on the elliptical machine in the small basement exercise room right before she called, or she's just that excited to hear about my *fabulosa* sartorial debut. Even odds on either one.

"Um, I guess. No one really said anything."

"Is because you refused to go with the sweater *I* preferred. The *naranja*. These grays and dark colors, they are not *especial* at all."

"There's nothing so *especial* about orange, Mom. You know I try to avoid wearing stuff that makes me look like a human citrus fruit."

A person should not have to justify these sorts of things, I think. The not-wanting-to-look-like-a-giant-grapefruit type of things. These are the kinds of things that should just generally go without saying.

She's quiet, so I forge blithely onward. "But, so. I was just about to call you, anyway. It turns out, I don't need you to pick me up. I've, uh, got a ride."

She shrieks louder than my Ricky Martin ringtone. "You made a friend!"

I choose not to dwell on the incredulity in her voice. "We met in homeroom. His name is Duncan. So, yeah."

Unspoken: *also, he has really cute eyes.*

"Ah, *sí*." Now she giggles like she can actually read my

mind, can pluck the image of his gemstone-hued peepers straight out of my brain. "Not to rush, then, *Agacita*. You don't need to come straight home."

"Right, but I think we probably will." Unless Duncan has secret plans to whisk me off to Paris for a romantic dinner for two. Which would be totally okay by me. My parents would never miss me, and I could shoot Chloe a text. If that were his secret plan, I mean.

Eh. Unlikely.

"Is not *problemo*, Aggie. I'm just going out to pick up something for dinner. Your papi, he says potatoes are good for the serotonin levels, but I tell him you need the protein for your energies."

She pronounces the *g* in *energies* like she's clearing her throat. When Mom is frazzled, her Spanglish tends to come out in full force. For the record, in a million years I would never call my father *Papi*. Never.

"Sounds great." I ignore the fact that I'm apparently facing a major carb ration on the home front, for now, because gemstone peepers are sparkling my way, and the rest of Duncan's body is following along with them. As bodies so often do.

"Gotta go. Love you."

I snap the phone shut. I glance up at Duncan.

And now I'm the one who's all breathless.

Duncan drives an SUV. It's a two-door, forest-green, one of those old-school Jeeps with the soft top that comes down— or completely off, I'm not sure which—in the summer. It seems a little impractical in a place like Denville, if you ask me, but I'm not about to break the fever-dream haze of being driven home by cuteness personified on my very first day of school by mentioning as much to him.

A hint of doubt must flicker across my face, though, because as he palms his car keys and clicks a quick alarm— *blipblip*—he laughs. The sound is bright and musical, and I find myself smiling back easily.

"It was a trade-off," he says. "The only truck I could afford, and it's a lot easier to layer up in winter than deal with something that doesn't have four-wheel drive."

"Right," I say, thinking again of Chloe and her BMW, which showed up in the driveway of her parents' condo on the morning of her sixteenth birthday, and which she has never had to drive in anything stronger than an unexpected sun shower.

"You're from Florida, right? Have you ever even seen snow?" He opens the driver's-side door and hops in, gesturing for me to do the same. (On the passenger side, I mean. Of course.)

I drop my messenger bag at my feet and shimmy the seat-belt harness over my torso. My jacket is buttoned up—even now, in October, it's plenty brisk out—but underneath it my tummy pooches out and strains against my waistband. Grossness. Remind me not to take Mom's advice again; my worn-in Levi's would have totally been just fine here, and eighteen times as comfortable, too. "Once. We were in New York City for Christmas. So that was cool."

"New York City. Please. That's minor leagues, Ag. You're going to faint from shock at the first sign of a real Denville winter."

Ag. He called me *Ag.* Like we're all friendly and old-time-y and nickname-y and stuff. Love it. *Love. It.* Even though he's essentially telling me I may want to consider hunkering down and hibernating through the upcoming season. Which, I'll admit, makes a lot of sense. Hibernation could very well be a solid plan. Remind me to look into that, later.

Duncan revs the engine, but just as he eases his hand over the gear shift, a pert dark head appears at his side, rapping on the soft, transparent plastic that serves as a window. He reaches up and unzips, in a gesture that strikes me as touchingly retro.

"Hey, Riley. What up?"

"I just wanted to remind you to pretty please bring the

notes from bio for me tomorrow." She smiles, flashing a row of teeth as perfect and precious as a strand of baby pearls. Something tells me this girl—*Riley*, I guess her name is—doesn't really need to resort to "pretty please's" to get what she wants. Even from where I sit, strapped against my seat with my hands tucked firmly under the flattened-out surface area of my upper thighs, I can just tell; this *Riley*, she oozes something, some kind of indefinable pheromone that temporarily renders the average high school student brain dead.

Riley is the kind of girl who reeks of charisma.

Chloe was that way, too. Back in Miami, she was. *Is*. But you know, back in Miami, I was Chloe's best friend. And that carried a hint of *eau de clout*, as well.

I should be smellier. If I'm going to make it here in Denville, I should flat-out stink of whatever snake oil causes otherwise immature adolescents to turn momentarily inside out at the sight of you.

Duncan nods, friendly and open, not impervious to the power of the precious pearl teeth. "From when you were out last week? I've got those. I'll bring 'em tomorrow. Definitely."

"You're the best," Riley squeaks, then bounces off to whatever A-list destiny surely awaits her. Squeaking and bouncing come naturally to girls like Riley.

She doesn't make it more than a few feet before she is nearly knocked to the ground by another student. Mind you, her assailant only offers a light hip check, but for a girl Riley's size, the slightest jostle could cause collapse. I'm pretty sure it's only the sheer force of will mixed with a healthy dose of caffeine—or maybe sugar (Would she eat sugar? *Hmm . . .*)—that keeps her in motion, generally speaking.

She laughs, tossing her hair back, and playfully shoves the guy who has crept up beside her. It takes me a moment to realize—it's the boy I saw at the diner. The one who made flannel look like a red-carpet fashion statement. The one who caused me to temporarily renounce my carnivorous ways just to score a few more seconds of Mom-free ogling. His hair is still the color of wet sand, floppy, shiny, and just long enough to be considered the slightest bit dangerous. There's a hint of danger to hair that long, and even if it's a sham, I want in. I do.

I'm embarrassed to admit that, passing my eyes over his lithe frame again, it's possible that I whimper. Audibly.

"Oh, man. Another one bites the dust."

I'd almost forgotten that I wasn't alone—clearly, or I'd be way more conscious of the trickle of drool that is no doubt making its way down my chin. I glance to my left at Duncan; he's taking full note of me as I admire Flannel-boy with a deep glimmer of hunger and lust, watching my eyes dance over the angles of the boy's body. I can't decide if I'm embarrassed at being caught gawping, or worried that I'm being rude to Duncan, who is plenty cute with a capital H-O-T in his own right. I'm so unschooled in these sorts of things, I'm practically remedial. I need another tutorial from Chloe, *stat*.

"What?" I'm trying to be cool—or, at least, lukewarm—but Flannel-boy's got me going worse than even Duncan's eyes could. Those overmuscled Miami Beach boys could take a lesson, here: sometimes less is more. Or, in the case of outerwear, I guess, *more* is more.

Whatever.

"Tobin. Tobin Young."

Ah. *Tobin.* Tobin Young.

His Indian name would be He Who Dresses Most Warmly and Regularly Conditions His Hair.

But *Tobin* will do just fine, too.

I say, "Oh." And I am temporarily satisfied that I have maybe kept the levels of "holy jumping beans" to a dull enough inner roar.

Nope. Duncan is *so* on to me. "Oh," he mimics, his voice skating a few octaves higher, teasing me. *"Oh."*

On the one hand, he doesn't seem to be offended, so at least I don't have to worry about the whole being-rude thing.

On the other hand, he's *definitely* making fun of me. Big-time.

He narrows a sly gaze at me. "I know that 'oh,'" he says. "That's the 'oh' that means that you want to have his little Tobin babies. And dress them up in little flannel footie pajamas. That's what that 'oh' is all about, my sister." He puckers his lips into an O for emphasis, and I involuntarily mock the gesture, giggling.

Little Tobin *babies*. Oh. Em. Gee. If Duncan only knew about my sad, romantic nonhistory. A full-frontal kiss from the dude would do just fine, thank you very much. So far, it's mostly been a sad peck here and there at the odd school dance or New Year's Eve party.

Thoughts of kissing, and Tobin, and Duncan, and kissing Tobin, and kissing Duncan, zip through my brain like lightning bolts. My head feels like a can of soda that someone's shaken all up, and it's suddenly very warm in the car. Can a person die, I wonder, from the presence of too much hot-itude?

It would be one H-E-double-you-know-what of a way to go. Right?

But still, I'd rather not. If given the option.

Duncan snorts again. I'm starting to recognize this as his signature move. He's lucky he's so cute. Generally speaking, snorting is not attractive, but he makes it work for him.

"You've got it bad, missy."

I shake my head. "You're crazy."

(He's not.)

He presses on. "I mean, Tobin has his fan club—hells, I heard a rumor about some girls who are thinking of starting a national chapter—but you? You have, like, some kind of weakened immune system to flannel. You are genetically predisposed to swoon in Tobin's general direction."

And now I have to snort-laugh myself. Because really, the boy has my number. And clearly he isn't hurt or offended in the least. Point to Aggie.

I guess I could be put out myself, if I really wanted to. I should, I suppose, want to be the type of girl who boys *would* get all worked up over. I should *want* Duncan to want me, to be irked to see me all wobbly and weak at the mere sight of Tobin's shoulders in profile.

And yet.

Maybe it goes back to my utter inexperience in all things guy related, but mostly I feel relieved. Because really, if nothing else, it's good to know that Duncan and I are going to be friends. Generally speaking, people try not to snort in front of other people if they are feeling remotely romantic toward said other people. This is a scientific fact. Generally speaking, snorting and kissing do not mix.

Which is probably a good thing, actually, seeing as how

being within ten feet of both Duncan and Tobin at the same time was shooting my core temperature up to volcanic-eruption levels. I can't imagine that's healthy.

"Are they—I mean, is she . . ." I can't bring myself to say the G word about Riley. Not in connection to Tobin. It's just, if I'm going to have to wrap my head around the fact that Duncan and I are already on a laugh-snort basis and potentially taking the express train to Platonic-ville, then I'm *definitely* not ready to learn that Tobin is already spoken for.

There's only so much disappointment a girl can take in a day, you know?

"Pfft," Duncan says, expanding his snorting repertoire rather impressively. "She wishes."

A tiny stain of hope blooms in my chest, filling up my rib cage like a balloon. "So he's single?"

Way to play it cool, Aggie.

Duncan rolls his eyes. "He's single." He finally turns his key in the ignition and lifts the parking break up. "And you're sad." But he's clearly teasing.

It's the kind of thing Chloe would say to me, like, if we were shopping or something. You know, after I'd tried on something skimpy, or wispy, and rushed to peel it off in fear, discomfort, or disgust. Which is why it doesn't offend me at all.

It's the truth: I *am* sad. And snorty, cute-faced Duncan gets that.

This is what's known in Aggie terms as *good news.*

Laughing together for real now, we slide smoothly back, out of the parking spot, my eyes locked on Tobin's figure as it shrinks along the horizon.

It feels really, really good to laugh for real.

And really, even shrunken down to a tiny pinpoint, Tobin is still pretty fine.

CHAPTER 7

The God of Bad Outfits is

laughing again. At me.

She's laughing—at *me*—and she's probably also forking a fiver over to the God of Bad Ideas, who I'm sure is having a hearty chuckle of his own at my expense right about now.

The first week of school passed painlessly enough; Tobin may not have shown any increased awareness of my existence, but then again, Duncan didn't show any decreased interest in being my friend. So the way I see it, I'm doing all right in the Great Series of Relocation Compromises.

But the weekend?

The weekend was hard. And weird. And unsettling.

To put it simply: *blech*.

In my personal experience, traditionally, weekends are a time for lounging poolside with Chloe, offering supportive feedback on her latest itsy-bitsy, teeny-weeny bikini, while furiously reknotting my sarong at my not-*not*-ample hips. Not for sending furtive texts in cell-phone shorthand to

Chloe, who couldn't possibly fathom the sight of a school full of kids dressed head to toe in L.L. Bean who weren't doing so for the sake of some sort of ill-conceived costume party.

Duncan had asked me if I maybe wanted to do the brunch thing with him and some friends on Saturday morning, but since that would have involved:

1) leaving the house,

2) making conversation with strangers,

and

3) probably also several other things I'm kind of slow to warm up to, I had to decline. It was enough that I'd put one foot in front of the other at school each day since we arrived in Denville, and responded—often with actual, coherent, and sometimes even correct— answers when teachers called on me in class.

But without plans with friends, or the motivation to reach out to Chloe (And how many times can you really type, MISS YOU!!! XOXO!!! before it starts to sound cliché, anyway? I'll tell you: not that many times. Not that many times at all.), by Sunday morning I was climbing the walls. Dad was in his study working on his first week's podcast for "Don't Be SAD—Spread Your Own Sunshine: Coping with Depression in Denville!" (I mean, can you *even*?), and Ricky Ricardo had taken to standing for hours on end with his round, wet nose pressed directly up against the space heater I'd set up in the family room. Neither of which were activities I particularly cared to join in on.

(Though I have to admit, that little portable heater *is* cozy. We've never had a fireplace or any need for an external source of heat before, and I can appreciate Ricky Ricardo's enthusiasm.)

The point of all of the above being that you can see how I was feeling especially vulnerable when Mom cornered me Saturday morning and invited me to join her at the *gimnasio*.

"I saw the advertisement on a board. At the supermarket."

I knew times had to be desperate indeed if Mom had taken to reading ads tacked up outside of the supermarket. Supermarket ads are really not Mom's style.

But, seriously—the *gym*? This had to be the worst mother-daughter bonding scheme of all time. Like, *Hi, Mom, have you met me? I'm your daughter, Aggie. The one who considers setting the dinner table to be adequate daily physical exertion. Often mistaken for a potted plant.* A quick eyebrow arch conveyed my doubt.

"There is an *e-spin* class," she went on, slightly more frantic, honey-blond locks bouncing high on her head in a perky ponytail. "We can ride the *bicicletas*." As if that were going to be the winning argument.

And yet.

In the end, it was the bouncing ponytail that got me. That, and a crippling lack of Anything Else to Do. Glancing toward the closed door of my father's office, I had to admit to myself that, actually, riding the *bicicletas* didn't sound completely horrific. Unfortunately, though, one of the things I hadn't bothered with, despite my increasing levels of boredom and restlessness, was unpacking in full.

Hence my current crime against honest, well-styled, Fashion Police–fearing people everywhere.

I'll say it again:

The God of Bad Outfits is laughing at me. She's laughing her *ass* off.

E-spin class in Denville, it would seem, is a little different than what Mom and I are used to back home in Miami. (Mom being more used to it than me, given my feelings on exercise.) And I'm pretty sure we're not what those fitness-conscious Alaskans had in mind, either.

I can't go into the real specifics about my outfit—it would be far too traumatic. Suffice it to say: *hot pink leggings. Capri, no less.*

Oh, yes. You heard me right. *Hot pink. Capri. Leggings.*

Classic rock blaring through the darkened studio, I catch a glimpse of myself in the long, mirrored wall that stands opposite the cluster of bikes. My whirring legs reflect the dim overhead lights, which would be kind of cool—that is, if I'd ever actually *wanted* to emulate a human disco ball.

Thankfully, the class instructor has managed to overlook my glittering, shimmering presence. I'm not sure how: the rest of the class is a sea of basic black track pants and drawstring shorts, coupled with straight-up Hanes-style T-shirts. None of those off-the-shoulder embellished tanks that Mom does so love to rock and, in fact, *is* rocking right now, at this very moment, to the rhythm of some full-on, major-league down-home guitar solos.

(Wherefore our techno club remixes? Wherefore our Spanish-language Christina Aguilera? This music is all bass and twang. No wonder these people are so freakin' depressed all the time.)

I grit my teeth as the muscles in my thighs tighten and pulse. Something about the image of my legs in the mirror, almost electric, has me hypnotized. I am the youngest person in this class, which wouldn't be a thing at all if my body weren't radiating like a beacon, or a bright, misshapen lighthouse at sea. Over my shoulder, Mom's reflection catches my own, and she winks. She's loving the fact that the two of us stand out, that we practically have our own personal spotlights trained on us. But then, Mom lives for theatrics.

Me, not so much.

The instructor screams something unintelligible that probably involves pedaling faster or upping the bike's resistance or otherwise doing something else that would only likewise up my current level of physical discomfort. I nod shortly, almost to myself, and reach down to the knob that controls the fly wheel's tension, pantomiming turning it up a notch or two. Congratulating myself silently for my brilliant subterfuge, I grab for the water bottle I've strapped into the holster at the side of my bike's frame.

(Hydration is *so* important, you know.)

I drink like a camel pre-Saharan trek, as though this is the first sip of water I've had in, like, forty-three years. I drink like I'm trying to drown myself. I can't take in enough, can't possibly quench my own thirst . . .

And then.

Gulping down heaping swallows of water, I am struck with a sudden and undeniable certainty:

I am going to yak.

Oh, barf.

Major, big-time barf. Like, literally.

I don't know if it's the pressure of the music bouncing off of the inside of my skull, or the flickering shadows my insane workout getup throws against the infinite reflection of the studio mirror. Or maybe it's the fact that I haven't exercised this hard since . . . well, since *ever,* really, and I just inhaled practically an entire bathtub of water.

Maybe, I think to myself, noting the sticky tendrils of hair plastered to the sides of my mirror-image's sweat-soaked face, *maybe I'm just sick of* myself.

That could be it. That could *totally* be it. Yeah. And also, *yeesh*.

But whatever. Regardless—like I say, it's an undeniable certainty: no matter the reason, the bottom line remains. If I don't get out of here, like, *immediately,* these shiny-cheeked, healthy, and totally unassuming citizens of Denville are going to be treated to an intense, up-close experience of the true "inner Aggie."

Clearly, nobody wants that.

I dismount the bike as gracefully as I can, which is to say, not very gracefully at all. The twenty-six minutes I spent spinning away seem to have reduced my legs to hollow twigs, to rubber, hardly substantial enough to support my slick, waterlogged, adrenaline-woozy frame. Mom shoots me a quizzical look, but I gesture in a way that tells her to stay put, not to worry. I wave my tote bag at her, shorthand for, *Text me when you're done, it's cool, we'll meet up.* And whether she gets it or not, she understands well enough that she doesn't follow me out of the studio and back onto Main Street, where I stumble along the sidewalk, gasping and hiccupping like nothing so much as the proverbial beached whale.

▃▁▅▆

Somehow, I don't barf. It must be a mind over matter thing. I manage to pull myself together while walking down Main Street, only to be quickly reminded that, in Denville, there are limited options available for a fugitive spin-class dropout wandering the streets on a random overcast Saturday morning, looking to kill time. The situation becomes all the more dire when I factor in my outfit—I'm dressed like a reject extra from an eighties music video, after all—and my sudden inability to stand upright for any extended period of time.

It's not good.

After quickly sizing up my alternatives, I duck into the diner, taking note that, according to signage that has (hopefully) seen better days, it does actually seem to be called, formally, The Diner. I can't believe I missed that weather beaten, scuffed, and rusted marquis up until now. This marks the second time I've visited this place, making it practically my regular hangout.

Back in Miami I had real, legit regular hangouts. Lots of them. Like, I couldn't even leave the house without hanging out, that's how many hangouts I had back home, in Miami. Okay, so mostly they were *Chloe*'s preferred hangouts, but still. They were regular. And that was a relief.

I settle myself at the counter and order a hot chocolate, then think better of it and order a ginger ale, too, for the barf factor. Mom probably wouldn't approve of either, but I can't be bothered to care. When she shows up, I'll just tell her ginger ale is diet, and the cocoa is coffee (she's okay with the idea that I could be stunting my growth with caffeine, but the sugar content in hot chocolate is a big Eckhart no-no, obviously).

The last time I heard from Chloe, she was IM'ing to tell me about Aaron Dallas's Homecoming after-party. Homecoming is still about six weeks away, but Aaron, being both the outgoing Homecoming king as well as a total shoo-in for this year's royal dude, went ahead and booked up a "phat" luxury suite at the Delano, where the junior and senior classes can go wild after the dance itself is over and done with.

(That's a direct quote. And no, I don't know why Chloe uses words like *phat*; I don't ask. Some things are better left unspoken.)

Party on, guys. I sniff, almost automatically.

Bitter? Jealous? Lonesome?

Me?

Never.

In some ways, Alaska is like a gift; I can curl up by myself on a shadowy, gray morning and not worry about anything other than blending fluidly, seamlessly, into my surroundings. Easier said than done when wearing hot pink leggings, sure—but don't underestimate my wallflower skills (*speaking* of gifts . . .).

I tip my face toward the mouth of my oversized mug, enjoying the warm, damp feel of the steam curling upward, kissing the contours of my face. Funny how just a few minutes ago I was three degrees away from overheating. This confirms my theories about the restorative powers of chocolate—I don't care what Mom thinks about net carbs or refined sugar. My stomach isn't even doing that twitchy Mexican-jumping-bean thing anymore. Progress, baby.

I pull my phone from the pocket of my cozy black fleece, still new and stiffer than I'd like, but well on its way to becoming a regular staple of my winter wardrobe. I never had much use for fleece, the fabric *or* the garment, back in Florida, but this pullover is like a reassuring hug. It's good stuff; between the fleece and the hot chocolate, I'm starting to feel a little more human again.

I scroll through my texts, mostly vague, uneventful missives from Chloe, who claims to miss me but seems to be doing just fine keeping busy in my absence (I'm *so* not bitter; I swear, I'm like the opposite of *bitter* in the dictionary).

And then, I remember:

My cell phone is *smart*. Like, smarter than I am, maybe even.

(Probably.)

Among its other fantastic and astounding talents—just yesterday, I tell you, it tied my shoes for me—my cell phone can read minds. It can send little electronic feelers out into the atmosphere, link up to whatever minuscule ionic charges Chloe's PDA is emitting, and it can tell me where in the world—where in my former *life*, really—she is. It can give me the precise coordinates of exactly where she currently sits (assuming she's sitting. But it could probably tell me where she's standing, too, if it were to turn out that she was actually standing right now). My cell phone can even print me up a full-on, 3-D, Technicolor topographical map of her surrounding environs. It can do all of that for *me—right now*. Right this *very second*.

Instant gratification. The absolute bestest kind of gratification there is.

If only I knew how to work my phone's GPS system.

I punch futilely at a few keys, which causes the screen to burst into a psychedelic display, but does not bring me any closer to pinning down Chloe's whereabouts.

I flip the device shut and drop it into my gold nylon gym bag (also Mom's, *obviously*). It's not like I really need a space-age piece of electronics to report back to me on what my friend is doing. I know her well enough, know Miami exactly well enough to know what's going down in my absence. Chloe probably went to a movie last night with

Tera and Devyn (also BFFs; they round out Chloe's little reign of love and lip gloss and butterflies). Maybe it was a romantic comedy, or something featuring one of the Wilson brothers. Then, probably, it was back to someone's house (I'm guessing Tera's; her parents are super-corny and always go hog wild with home-cooked brunch in the morning) for gossip, Red Vines, and sleepover antics (Chloe likes to "chillax" on Fridays; Saturday was always our typical party night).

If I squeeze my eyes shut tightly enough, I can smell the sharp, acrid burn of nail polish remover, can hear the clack of Tera's keyboard as she dashes off IMs to her latest crush while we girlies gab away. See, cell phone? Who even needs you and your awesome powers of surveillance?

Not me. Nope. Not one little bit.

Faced with the current state of eventlessness in my own life, I have no recourse but to retreat into the world of celebrity slander—uh, I mean, *gossip*. *Us* magazine should do just fine. Fortunately, I never leave home without it. I grab it from my bag and flip away eagerly, happy for a temporary escape.

But. *Eeehh*; it's all just the same old crap as last week, and the week before that, and the week before that: some blond pop star has gotten "fat"; someone else is hidden away on a private island, either detoxing or possibly getting new boobs. Someone got a tattoo this week that means "wind" in ancient cuneiform. Someone is thinking of adopting a baby, or maybe a pot-bellied pig.

I reach for my mug of hot chocolate, but it's cooled considerably during my brief pity party. I look up to catch the waitress's eye, the same woman from dinner the other night, with the Ronald McDonald hair, but she's distracted, pencil clenched between her harshly outlined lips, rolling the lip of a paper bag closed for a to-go order.

"Thanks, Cady." The voice is smooth and warm, better than a refill of hot chocolate. *Way* better.

The voice is Tobin's.

The realization is so sharp, so sudden, that my breath catches just in the base of my stomach. It's still the best I've felt all morning, but that's no help; powerless, I begin to slide backward on my slick, pleather barstool, managing only a quick mental, *Oh, please, no*, before my center of gravity completely inverts.

In a split second, it hits me: the God of Bad Outfits has consulted with the Fairy Prince of Ironic Timing. I may have been spared the full-on yak-fest, but I'm going down.

And then.

There's a firm hand pressed solidly against my back, steady against the quivery space between my shoulder blades, radiating energy and balance and calm. It takes me a moment to assess, to confirm: I am, indeed, upright. The floor is beneath me, as floors are meant to be.

I'm wavering, trying to decide what the appropriate response is to the person who has just prevented my second most humiliating experience of the day, when Ironic Timing Guy finally, *finally* cuts me a break, and Tobin turns to face me.

"I saved your life." His wide, easy smile is enough to make me renounce processed sugar entirely, no joke. In all of my sixteen years, I had no idea that such smiles existed. This is a scientific discovery on par with penicillin, or fat-free frozen yogurt. Chloe would be so proud.

"Stools are tricky," I offer, flushing. "With the plastic and the . . . slippy-ness . . ."

"Well, and those pants look kind of . . . challenging."

The *pants*. Right. I'm still wearing the "Like a Virgin" leggings. Just kill me now.

"Spin," I offer weakly. As if there could possibly be any legitimate explanation for pants like these.

"Right, spin. Workout Woman," Tobin says, running his hand through a flip of wavy hair. "My mom does that class. I was gonna meet her after, take some lunch over to my dad, at work, on our way home." He nods toward the paper bag that Cady has prepared and slid his way.

"Yeah, um, I . . . cut out early." Just in time, it occurs to me not to share the details of my near detour to Puke-ville with this perfect, pristine specimen of a teenage boy.

He smiles again, crinkling the corners of his eyes. "I probably would, too. The whole idea of indoor cycling sounds sort of dumb to me. Biking to nowhere, you know? I mean—no offense," he adds.

I want to agree, but doing so might imply that I'm actually the type who prefers hiking to *somewhere*, when, as we all know, I'm really the type who prefers a good, long lounge when it comes to my leisure "activities." So I settle for a grin and a light, "None taken."

"Look," he says, and I think he's gearing up for something major, or at least major-*ish*. But then he points out the window of the diner like he really wants me to *look* look, not *listen* look. "I think that's them."

I follow his index finger to see two women, one of whom sports a close-cropped pixie cut the exact shade of Tobin's mop-top and a sweatband that runs the circumference of her delicately damp forehead. Next to her is my mother, sparkle lip gloss gleaming almost as brightly as her bedazzled hoodie. They are like a photo essay on opposites. Nonetheless, they're chatting easily with each other, postures relaxed and natural, the recent proof of Mom's awesome talent at winning people over. That's the good news.

The bad news is that at any moment, they're going

to charge in here, my mother hovering and fretting and pecking and generally making me look even more socially incompetent in front of Tobin than I already do. This is profoundly Not Okay.

I have to act fast.

This time, I scoot off of my stool deliberately, landing on the ground with a small bounce and slinging my bag over my shoulder.

"I should run," I say, like I have eighty-nine things to cross off my to-do list today. Like there's a cotillion, or a house party, or a fairy-tale ball awaiting me, a crowd of festive partygoers just hanging on the promise of my arrival. Anything other, better . . . *more* . . . than a bilingual rat dog, a space heater, and a cell phone that keeps closer tabs on my old friends than I do.

"Right, yeah," he says, politely not calling bull crap on my social butterfly act.

And then he says, "I'll see you at school, Aggie."

He'll see me. At school.

Why, yes. Yes, you will.

I float through the door toward my mother, not even minding the knit in her eyebrows as she notes the trace of cocoa residue dotting the corner of my mouth. Letting her admonishments about bailing on *e-spin* class roll straight down my back like a cool, refreshing waterfall. Nothing that she or any of the creative, colorful Powers That Be throw at me can possibly take away from my one small—but meaty—triumph.

Tobin Young knows my name.

Even in my disco-queen outfit. Even with the vertigo that comes from hopping up and down off of various unstable forms of seating.

Even with all of that, I'm still totally *e-spinning*.

For Halloween, Ricky Ricardo

is dressed as a caballero out of the Wild, Wild West—complete with holster and fringed vest—and I renew my long-standing love affair with Reese's Peanut Butter Cups. Mom busts out the aforementioned digital camera that the network gave her as a retirement present and makes like a possessed William Wegman. We reach a shaky compromise, she and I, wherein she agrees to turn a blind eye to my candy consumption for as long as I assist—snark-free—in styling for her shoot. And while it's not easy to shut down the snark, I discover, I do decide that it is ultimately worth it.

The whole ordeal is like an acid trip—minus the acid—but strangely enough, it works for me.

Sunset has crept back to six o'clock, and trick-or-treaters descend upon us early. Another shocker: it's *fun* watching a revolving parade of costumed children wobble eagerly toward our door in humming clusters, an entirely different experience than what we're used to from our high-rise back home. I know I haven't been a huge champion of the weather in Denville, but there's something appropriately autumnal about the bare branches that form latticework against the gray sky. The air is crisp, which never happens along the soupy shore of the Atlantic.

It makes me smile to see trick-or-treaters try to reconcile their costumes with the chill in the air; the miniature ghosts with long johns peeking out from beneath their bedsheets, and the tiny teacup witches shrouded in dark wool cloaks. Where does one get a cloak in a size that small? I wonder. The kids get a kick out of our dressed-up dog, and Mom's corresponding Ye Olde Barmaid getup, too, and the validation is enough to keep my straight-shootin' mama giddy and giggling for hours. The ratings from Dad's latest show are strong, better than his agent's wildest projections, and there was even a feature on him in last week's *Sun* that got picked up by the AP. Our phone's been ringing off the hook since that one ran, making for a fairly delicious Halloween treat for us all.

But all of this tricky tomfoolery can last for only so long. Once the after-school crowd drifts away, I head to my room to think about homework. I'm supposed to be reading Toni Morrison, but I'm feeling a little more like getting my *Flashdance* on. Talk about your old-school chick flick. And besides, I'm totally keeping on theme—it's Halloween, after all, and leg warmers are very scary stuff.

Right?

I curl up in bed amid an explosion of patterned throw pillows. Mom was in charge of decorating the new place, and offering any input would have been like tacitly acquiescing to our Arctic expedition. My own choice in bedclothes would involve far fewer . . . well, bedclothes, honestly, but I have to admit, it's pretty comfy here, throws tossed haphazardly into inviting lumps of squishy, scrunchy cushioning. It's the ideal cocoon for spending some quality time with my classic DVD collection.

What a feeling, folks. Really.

·ıl

So apparently the eighties were a very confusing time, both for fashion and also for the burgeoning go-go dance movement. This is what I've learned from *Flashdance*. The female welder has just screwed her courage together and decided to pursue an audition for the snooty ballet company—you go, girl!—when the door to my bedroom squeaks open a notch.

"Oh my god, are you actually watching *Flashdance*? That. Is. *Awesome*. You should have called me."

Duncan. Is here. In my house.

Oh.

I take a moment to thank whatever incredible psychic foresight prevented me from putting on the threadbare PINK sweatpants with the hole right under my left butt cheek. (It's the little things, really.) I straighten up on my bed as best as I can, which is harder than you might think, given that the surface of the bed is at least 70 percent pillow and other cushiony matter. I try to give Duncan my most serious expression, despite the fact that I *am* wearing the ratty velour pants with the crusty fro-yo stain on the right thigh, and I'm drowning in an overstuffed sea of—it must be noted—*very* well-coordinated bedding.

Cute-faced boys should really not be allowed to call upon unsuspecting females this way. I'm just saying.

"What are you doing here?" I push myself up and off of my bed—also much more of a challenge than one might expect—and place my laptop on my desk, stopping the movie just before the welder freaks out and flees from the ballet school admissions office. She's having a major crisis of confidence.

I can relate.

"Yeah, great to see you, too," he replies, arching an eyebrow at me. "Your mom let me in. I'm digging that fringed vest she's wearing."

I groan. I know that Dunc and I have been cruising in the Friend Zone of late, but is it necessary for me to be so thoroughly humiliated during the course of his impromptu visit? "I wish I could tell you that it was, like, a fashion anomaly, but she actually grabbed it out of her everyday rotation and repurposed it special for her Halloween costume. *Repurposed.* Like, this is the vest's *second* purpose in its fast-paced, thrill-ride of a short, vest-y little life."

"How industrious of Mom," Duncan quips. "And how exhilarating for little Vesty."

"There's a fine line between industry and insanity." I should know. She's *my* mother.

"Aggie"—Duncan tsks—"no need to poop the party. At least your mom's got a personality. That's more than I can say for half the people populating this crazy carousel of a planet. And anyway, if you can't get wild on Halloween, when can you?" He collapses into a lavender corduroy beanbag chair, eyes widening briefly in alarm as the fabric threatens to swallow him up.

"Right," I say. "That's just it—I'm not one for getting wild." Can you say, *understatement of the millennium*?

"Pity," he replies. "I was hoping I could bring out your secret animal instinct. But that dream hinged on the assumption that you actually had some." He nods in a way that suggests that he's made up his mind about some unspoken fact. "Now.

I do love me some Jennifer Beals, *natch,* so I'm willing to spare some time for this little social detour, but I think we're going to have to turn the volume up, doll. Didn't your mama ever teach you to share your toys?"

Huh? "Animal instinct?" I'm still stuck on that. I consider it in the abstract, drawing two incontrovertible conclusions:

1) No, as a matter of fact, I do *not* have any. *Nada* by way of animal instinct. In point of fact, I am the exact, precise opposite of wild. That's, like, the whole *thing* about me. Or, not-thing, I suppose.

And also:

2) I have no idea what in the name of jeezum he's going on about. Somewhere along the road, I seem to have lost my way amid the winding cobblestones of our rapid-fire, witty banter.

Duncan leans forward, the contours of the beanbag chair shifting beneath him. He wobbles slightly but manages to reach for his messenger bag, from which he pulls out two sets of wiggling alien antennae headbands. They twinkle a glittery shade of chartreuse at me. Saucy!

"Aliens? I thought you said *animal* instinct." Clarity is still elusive. Though one thing's for sure—it ain't a date if he's wearing a headband. No boy would demean himself that way in front of a true crush. Or so I presume, in the absence of definitive empirical research.

Duncan shrugs. "Draw some whiskers on your cheeks, you're an alien cat. Gold."

Riiight. "Um. As much as I enjoy your unexpected visit, Dunc, I have to tell you, I have no idea what you're going on about." And I'm wishing I had known he was coming over; this is his first time at my house, and leaving aside the whole dirty drawstring pants issue, I would have at least tossed yesterday's discarded Ruby Gloom socks into the hamper if I'd been expecting company. It's a good thing I'm saving myself for Tobin Young, in theory.

Anyway. The purpose of his visit. Sometimes the shortest distance between two points is a straight line, or so I hear.

Duncan says, "There's a party," and I freeze.

I mean, I don't want to be presumptuous, and I'm sure I'm totally reading too much into it, but . . . still . . . maybe . . . I have to wonder . . .

Is Duncan kind of asking me out?

Nu-uh. No way. This is just his being nice to the new girl, the same way he was just being thoughtful—and maybe even, a little bit, pitying me—when he invited me to brunch with his friends.

Like Tobin, guys like Duncan—cute-faced guys, that is—don't go for girls like me. They don't go for girls in holey sweatpants. They go for girls like Chloe. Or Riley. Girls who don't know from double-digit clothing sizes.

Regardless, a party with scads of strangers—possibly even our whole entire junior class—seems like way more than I'm ready for.

"Tegan Darcy is having a party tonight. I'm meeting a bunch of folks there. You're going."

Aha. *There* it is. I was right: it's a friend-date invite. "Bunch of folks" is practically code for the friend-date invite.

I can't decide whether to relax or deflate. In the end, I compromise: *both!*

I haven't really spoken to Tegan Darcy too much, but of course, I know who she is. Denville just isn't that big, and she hangs with Riley and Tobin and their crowd, all of whom seem to be jock-y and into sports and fitness and other wacky things pertaining to being healthy. Whereas I am into chocolate and peanut butter and other things pertaining to leaving my bedroom as infrequently as possible. Like, I know Duncan is much more social than I am (not exactly a huge accomplishment—your average goldfish is more social than I am, when I'm not flanking Chloe or my other Miami co-minions), but that doesn't mean that I have to go along with his crazy schemes. Does it?

I mean, really: an *alien cat*?

"You're not busy." He states the obvious.

I shrug. "Shows what you know. I happen to be *extremely*

preoccupied with the very urgent task of stalking my Florida friends online while *they* do the whole Halloween-party thang." And also: picking at the stain on my pants. So.

Now Duncan crosses to where I sit and lowers himself next to me, scootching me over a few paces and bumping his shoulder against mine in a way that feels familiar, reassuring.

The Friend Zone isn't the worst place to be, I think. Sometimes a friend is a comforting thing.

"Agatha Eckhart," he begins again, looking stern.

So much for "comforting." I brace myself.

"While I heartily approve of your use of the term *thang*, dearie, the idea of you frantically *stalking*—to use your word—your friends back home when you *could* be out bingeing on pumpkin beer and fun-sized Snickers yourself is simply too depressing to bear. I can't allow my best girl to indulge in such lame-osity. Frankly, it reflects poorly on me."

Hearing Duncan call me his best girl gives me a nice flash of the warm fuzzies, but please. It's still not enough to coax me out of my pj's and into pants that actually zip or button. Not by a long shot. Maybe it'd be different if he called me a sex goddess, but that's clearly not in the cards.

I reach for the computer I abandoned, rest it on my knees, and tap quickly at the keyboard. The screen fills with light. Duncan hovers over my shoulder, scanning the map that

I've called up. It's a rooftop party space in South Beach. It's also where Chloe et al. are showing off their Halloween costumes (slutty nurse? or slutty vampire? or—hey!— maybe even slutty French maid!) while they get themselves into all sorts of typical teen trouble.

"This is where your friends are?" he confirms. I nod.

I can tell he's impressed. Who wouldn't be? The party is on par with some of those that J-Lo herself has thrown on my former stomping grounds. But he covers, pressing his lips together tightly.

"Looks great, Ag," he says, gently taking the computer from me and closing it firmly. It's a MacBook Air: light, slender, trendy. Even my computer is sleeker, more stream-lined, all around better-looking than I am.

Duncan goes on. "But Aggie, you're *here*. Alaska. Which is basically the opposite of Florida. Time to start owning it." He breathes deeply, and I know that he's equal parts teasing me and meaning what he's saying.

I kind of like that he can do both at the same time.

"What'd you do, anyway? Set up a live webcam to follow them?" he asks.

"No, creepy-pants," I say, offended. "I'm not *that* much of a weirdo loser."

(I'm *not*, you know.)

(Well, not *really*.)

I sigh. "My phone has GPS. If I 'pin' Chloe, it tracks her and sends her coordinates to a special Web site."

"Ah." He nods sagely. "A special Web site for sad shut-ins who never leave their houses and live vicariously through the adventures of others. Groovy."

Ah, indeed. Not to put *too* fine a point on it.

"It's a valid lifestyle choice." Because, see, it totally *is*. I cross my arms over my chest in a huff.

He tilts so that he's facing me, puts a hand on my knee. "I'm not gonna *force* you to come with me, Aggie."

Well. *That's* a relief. Problem solved!

"Okay! In that case, I hope you have a good time," I say. I have a movie to get back to, anyway—I need to know if the welder ends up following her dreams and her heart.

I do hope Duncan has a good time, though—really, really, I do; I have nothing against parties. In fact, I did enjoy a good one often enough back home. But that was when I had my reinforcements firmly in place: Chloe, Tera, Devyn. Here, I've got Duncan, and yeah, he's been completely awesome— how amazing of him to come by to see if I would go out with him, right? But *Duncan Reid: the relative awesomeness thereof,* doesn't change the fact that Denville is a totally new social landscape. And it certainly doesn't change the fact that there's no way in ell-hay I stand a chance with Tobin Young. And therefore, by extension, it doesn't change the incontrovertible fact that I have no real reason to rouse myself for the sake of this party.

We go back and forth for a little while longer, but once Duncan realizes that I am serious about wanting to stay in (and also, that I am shockingly impervious to his considerable charms), he gives me a friendly hug and bids me farewell. I am his best girl, after all.

I shrink back into the warmth of my bed and watch him retreat from the room. His alien antennae, which he donned surreptitiously at some unnoticed point in his visit, bob like buoys in his wake.

It's kind of wild.

.ıl

After he's gone, I reach for my quilted satin coverlet, pulling the edge up underneath my chin and inhaling the clean scent of laundry detergent and my mother's body moisturizer. He might not have realized it—*I* might not even have realized it until exactly this moment—but Duncan's surprise visit made me feel all glowy and lit up from the inside. It hits me in full: this has been the first night since we arrived in Denville that nightfall dipped over me like candle wax, pleasantly surreal and malleable, instead of the abrupt, inky cover I've come to expect and dread.

Duncan's rad; I can already tell that I like him as well as any of my old friends, even if his face *is* heart palpitation–inducing.

(Side note: CuteFace can be dangerous to your health!)

But anyway. Something about the way Duncan rested his shoulder against my own felt real in a way that almost nothing ever does, like the color of a pristine stretch of lawn after a heavy rainfall, a deluge. But I'm still not sorry I didn't go with him to the party tonight. I'm reveling in the downtime, in the cave I've built here in my bedroom. And I'm kind of thinking that that's A-okay.

Duncan's love of classic eighties movies may earn him a thousand bonus points in the game show that is my life, but it doesn't mean that we're at the stage, he and I, where he becomes my own personal night-light, my miner's cap. My jack-o'-lantern. I had that with Chloe, and yeah, it was comfortable.

But.

Something about this place, the cold, the white—it's all a blank slate. A chance to reconsider my own negative space. Here in Alaska, I'm taking a beat. A pause. Feeling things out. Reflecting, like the glassy surface of a smooth sheet of ice.

Duncan is a brilliant prism, even more than Chloe was. (Sorry, C., but it's true.) She was—*is*—white light, but

Duncan's got every color in the spectrum illuminating his frame. He's translucent. Incandescent.

And Denville? Denville throws shadows. They hug me, pull me in.

Maybe at some point, my wild-alien-animal glitter-girl will shake her way out of my skin. Maybe. But for now, the whole hibernation thing is working for me. I'm not quite ready to emerge from the shadows.

Not yet.

.ıil

Something strange comes over me that night, though; I don't even get it myself. But for some unfathomable reason, when Mom calls up to me that it's time to eat dinner, I decide to wear my antennae to the table. Mom catches my eye over a heaping wooden serving bowl of salad and winks. Dad raises a curious eyebrow. He doesn't comment, but he does seem amused. I'm amused, too.

Even Ricky Ricardo seems to approve.

Can you blame him?

CHAPTER 9

If I ever become the Official

Queen and Ultimate Ruler of the Universe, I swear to the Powers of Marshmallow and Graham Cracker, the very first thing I'm going to do will be to abolish phys ed class for all eternity.

I am *so* not kidding, people.

Sure, we had gym class back in Miami—I spent that period "running" laps with Chloe around our outdoor track and offering sage advice on her latest romantic entanglement. It was a great arrangement, Chloe being adept with the dating and boy-things, and me being adept with the listening-and-nodding-things.

Gym is different here in Denville.

For starters, it's *cold* outside. I think I might have mentioned that once or twice before.

In Miami, the advent of November means cooler temperatures, closed-toed shoes, and an umbrella in your bag at all times. It means seventy-five degrees if you're lucky, the low sixties if you aren't.

I used to think a rainy November day in Miami was the worst.

It turns out, I thought wrong.

In Denville, we wear thermal underwear underneath our regulation-issue gym uniforms. It itches. I didn't know underwear could itch. And frankly, the ignorance was a blessing.

Also: our gym teacher, Coach Franklin, seems to regard me as a curiosity of sorts. On my first day, she swept her eyes over me, taking in the curve of my hips in my skinny jeans and the slight softness of the underside of my chin, and clearly determined that I was weak. Coddled. Nothing like the hearty, rugged athletes she sees year in and year out, kids who *look forward* to snow and even voluntarily participate in outdoor winter sports.

She was right about that—my interest in, for example, ice-skating waned once I hit the age of six—but I'm still not thrilled with the suspicious glares she sneaks toward me while we run hockey drills.

I mean, I'm doing my best.

"OMG, spazz much?"

"Huh?"

Okay, so my best is really not that impressive. I'll admit

it. Still, there's no cause for such attitude. I look up from my hockey stick to see Tegan Darcy, she of the Halloween parties and Duncan's acquaintance, eyeing me with disdain.

At least it's *so* cold today that we're inside for class, practicing our passes on the polished surface of the basketball court. Still, I would have thought that it would be easier for a novice like myself to control a puck (really a little round ball, but whatever, same diff; *I told you I'm not an athlete, people*) without a sleek sheet of ice to contend with.

Shows you what I know.

"Sorry," I mumble to Tegan, even as I wonder who exactly sneezed in her Fruity Pebbles this morning. She just sighs and darts off in the direction of the puck.

I've never been much for darting myself. I'm much more of an ambler, you know? I glance around, disheartened, to find Duncan shooting me a sympathetic glance from across the basketball court, where the boys are practicing, their movements mirroring our own. I bet he's thinking, *I told you so*. I bet he's thinking, *You and Tegan would be besties by now if you'd only gone to her Halloween party*.

Halloween was on Friday, and so was Tegan Darcy's party. On Saturday, Duncan texted to tell me that it was a rager, that Tegan *almost* exchanged digits with a guy from the Farmingdale cross-country ski team there. Some party crasher or whatever. I texted him back to ask what exactly "almost" exchanging digits would consist of. His reply was a sly emoticon wink that elucidated nothing.

That little snatch of gossip reminded me that cross-country skiing is, like, a Thing here. It's a whole Big Deal here in Denville. That, in point of fact, there is an entire section coming up on cross-country in phys ed this month. Or so Coach Franklin told us.

I have a feeling she wasn't kidding. Coach Franklin hardly seems like the kidding type. Or, I mean, maybe it's her excessive facial hair that is the true cause of her perma-scowl, but the point being: winter sports.

The thought of donning ski pants and strapping the equivalent of two polished wooden rails to my legs makes me slightly queasy. Or that could be a sugar hangover from one too many Halloween Reese's (though I strongly assert that there's really no such thing as too many when it comes to individually wrapped chocolate treats), or the side effects of all of this physical exertion.

Spazzing takes a lot of effort, people.

It's too bad about that almost-exchange of numbers, though. Maybe Tegan would be acting a wee bit less premenstrual if she'd managed to lock down the potential hookup. Like, we'd be weaving each other friendship bracelets and stuff, and Duncan wouldn't have to look so baleful from all the way across the cavernous gymnasium.

Please. As if I even care. Like I even would *want* to be besties with someone who constantly looks like she's been caught in the act of smelling something foul.

Coach Franklin blows her whistle and I start, shuffling quickly toward the cluster of stick-wielding girls. In the center of the melee, Riley Townsend (yes, of course that's her last name—did you doubt for a second that her name would be any less stately and stage-name sounding than that?) winds her arms in a graceful arc, sending the puck in a deliberate trajectory, as if it's an extension of her own brain.

Everything about Riley is effortless and graceful, I'm learning. It's . . . impressive. And intimidating. She's kind of nice, too. Which makes it nearly impossible to resent her. Though I promise you, I'm trying my darnedest.

Later, when the period ends, Riley jogs up alongside Tobin and elbows him in the ribs. He grins at her and offers her a high five. I suddenly feel like I've been punched in the stomach, but I truly think I cover admirably.

I don't even realize I'm watching the two of them, Tobin and Riley, partners in perfection, wistfully and maybe not a little bit creepily, until Tegan's face pops out in front of my own all over again.

She smirks. "They're totally getting back together," she informs me, righteous, which is so much more information than I needed and causes my throat to tighten in sympathy. It's like I'm having an allergic reaction to the fact of Riley and Tobin.

Tegan can see the strain on my face, the disappointment. I'm sure of it. And I swear she looks happy.

I am so not fooling anyone here. Not one little bit.

Least of all, myself.

.ıl

And then. It gets colder, even.

Mornings are the worst. Mornings are when you step outside and the cold is like a frigid fist. It grabs hold of your lungs and squeezes like it's trying to choke the life back into you.

I like it.

No lie. For some strange reason, I kind of like it.

Especially on the weekends, when there's nowhere in particular that I have to be, when I can snuggle farther under my comforter and get comforter-able, despite the icicles forming in our drainpipes, and the fact that Bored Mom has designs of making me her photography assistant, or intern, or indentured servant or something.

My alarm blares. Soothing. I glance at the screen of my cell phone again to check the time: eleven-thirty. Okay, I'm done with the snooze button for the day. Thank the God of Small Favors, Mom is back at *e-spin* class (we both agreed that I'm just not cut out for the Spin), and Dad told me he would be "culling some data" all over the dining room table today.

(Side note: *culling data* looks an awful lot like *listening to classic jazz and drinking cran-apple juice*, but, hey, what do I know about psychology?)

My windowpanes are frosted, speckled with dots of ice crystals that suddenly look as inviting to me as a sandy beach.

Enough of this room. I need some fresh air.

I decide on something desperate.

Something unexpected.

Something Chloe would never, ever have seen coming.

I decide to go for a walk.

I throw on some silk long johns (way less itchy than thermals), insulated nylon pants, a long-sleeved fleece top, and my puffy jacket. With this much padding, I could face-plant into a snowdrift and probably survive several decades or so, but the overall effect is soothing and cocoonlike, as though I were still tucked warmly in bed—if it weren't for how I am standing upright, and also, you know, outside of the house.

Dad asked me where I was walking to and seemed unconcerned when I told him that I didn't know, which I didn't. I promised him I'd take my phone, which is, as we all know, more reliable than a bloodhound.

Now that I'm outside, my body seems to have a brain of its own, wholly independent from the one that's in my head and sends me messages on a (semi)regular basis. I push smoothly along, muscles contracting against the chill and straining as I follow the gentle slope down, away from the residential area of Denville. I don't even realize that I am moving steadily toward town until I find myself smack dab in the center of it, across from the diner and adjacent to the workout studio that we all remember as being the site of my abject humiliation.

(I'd prefer not to talk about the near-barf experience, okay? A little consideration, please.)

My heart is doing jumping jacks inside of my throat, and I can feel a damp trickle of sweat building up at the waistband of my pants. But more than anything physical, what I feel is surprise that I've arrived here. Not that town is so far from our house—homes radiate outward from the town center like spokes on a wagon wheel—but still. I've probably walked a mile. Downhill, yeah, but *still. A mile.* Completely of my own free will, and for no good reason other than a mild attack of sudden-onset boredom.

How about that?

I am standing in the middle of the sidewalk, marveling at the triumphant, agile athlete I've become—*eat your collective, skinny little hearts out, Monroeville cross-country team!*—when I hear my name. I pop my head up, snapping out of the fantasy in which I graciously accept the Olympic Gold Medal in the category of archery (kind of random, I know, but—archery! Neat-o).

It's Tobin. Tobin Young. Of the shaggy hair that screams to be twirled around girl fingers. *My* fingers, to be exact. He smiles, moves fluidly toward me, a to go bag from the diner tucked neatly in the crook of his elbow.

Oh, to be a to-go bag tucked neatly in the crook of *Tobin Young's* elbow . . .

Sigh.

It occurs to me that the diner is practically our place by now. I mean, he probably came here looking for me in the first place. Right?

I say, "Hey." Because I'm cool like that. I try to push the thought that I am wearing enough clothing to moonlight as my own life raft out of my mind. I try to pretend that Tegan Darcy never told me that Tobin is spoken for, that Riley has dibs.

Even if I were, somehow, through some alternate-universe wormhole, able to become the type of girl who usually gets a guy like Tobin? Even if that were, against all odds, a fact?

Even in that most unlikely scenario, I'd still never be able to compete with someone like Riley. Because, let's face it: shiny black hair . . . grace . . . and, apparently, a history with Tobin, too.

Riley Townsend, people. Remember?

Tobin says, "We have to stop meeting like this," and it's not corny or cliché when *he* says it, and also, his left front tooth is the tiniest bit crooked in a way that makes it 139 percent impossible not to lurve him even more, *Riley Townsend* or no. I laugh.

"Lunch?" I ask, shrugging my shoulder at his bag o' takeout, because in addition to being the very embodiment, the absolute *essence* of coolness, I am also: Mistress of the Obvious Statement.

"Yeah," he agrees, politely not commenting on how I am so very definitely having a neurological event just as a result of being in his most electrified presence, and really, it's embarrassing for both of us. "But—oh, I mean, it's not for me."

"Right," I say, because it's my turn in the conversation, and "right" seems like a fairly appropriate contribution. It totally seems like something to say, until you realize that there's an implication there, a suggestion that of course—of *course*—I know exactly where that food is going. Of *course* it's not for my good buddy and lifelong soul mate, the person whom I know inside and out, Tobin Young.

Of course not.

I totally knew that.

"I take lunch to my dad on Saturdays. It's his busiest day," he goes on, still like we're besties, still like I have any idea what in the holy whoosiwhatsie he's talking about.

"Saturdays are busy," I say, and at this point, I'm not even trying to pretend I'm doing anything other than parroting key phrases back at him. The last time I was struck by this degree of crazy-pants was when I first met Duncan. I'm sensing a trend here. Can you be vaccinated for immunity to Cute Boy Swoonage syndrome? 'Cause I'm pretty sure it's, like, a real thing.

"Tours are pretty much back-to-back on weekends, and especially Saturdays. All of the Anchorage tourists spill out here for dogsled tours."

His father runs dogsled tours? For Anchorage tourists? That's . . .

Well, that's kind of weird. But in a cool, interesting way.

"I know," he says, as if I've actually said something out loud. "It's weird."

The boy can read my mind. That's a definite sign of how we are soul mates. *Definitely.*

"No, it's cool," I protest. I mean, on Tobin, weirdness

takes on a whole different aura. It's that special, scientific charisma pheromone again. "I always thought . . ." I trail off. "I guess I don't know what I always thought about dogsleds." Because if we're going to be really brutally honest about it, dogsleds aren't something I've ever given a whole lot of thought to. I've never had reason to, until this very exact, precise moment in time.

Suddenly, I urgently regret my lack of dogsled-related introspection. All of that time spent tracking various celebrity pregnancies could *so* have been put to better use.

"Your mother," Tobin says, which seems like the absolute biggest non sequitur in the entire world history of a boy and girl talking, until I follow his gaze over my shoulder and see my mother, much as Tobin indicated, moving toward me with terrifying briskness.

Once she reaches me, she swoops down and envelops me so that her sticky, *e-spin*-fresh cheek presses against my own. It's slightly icky, but also a little warm and alive, like how I felt when I found myself having walked all the way into town.

"*Agacita!*" she exclaims with delight, causing me to cringe. "I'm glad you're here. You must have read my brain. We need to pick up your *equipage para* the cross-country *e-ski*!" She beams at Tobin. "Your guidance counselor tells me there is an *e-ski* session in the *gym* class. Do you *e-ski*?"

Tobin nods shyly, a quick dip of the head. He has somehow managed to wade through Mom's broken Spanglish. Major bonus points. "I'm on the school ski team. Cross-country."

"*Perfecto!*" Mom exclaims, as though he's just told her he possesses the ability to raise television soap ratings merely via the powers of his mind. "You can help Aggie to learn."

Holy jeezum! Mortification alert, code level: ultraviolet. Is Mom actually trying to pick up my *objet d'affection for me?*

There are no words. None.

I am trying to decide when and by what method I will be murdering my mother in her sleep when Tobin chuckles. The sound is the aural equivalent of the way an icy Coca-Cola tastes in your mouth when imbibed upon arriving at a Fourth of July pool party. Which is to say: *utterly and extremely fabulicious.*

"Anytime," Tobin says, the word rolling smoothly off of his tongue.

So, Mom gets to live another day.

Anytime.

The hope that he means it is a deep, almost physical ache in that hollow space where my ribs come together in my chest. *Anytime.*

"Your mama, she stayed behind to talk to the *e-spin*

teacher, but she will be coming out soon to go with you to the dogsled place, to meet your father with his lunch," Mom assures Tobin, and side note: I cannot believe how much more my mother knows about Tobin's life than I do. Never mind calling off the mob hit: I should really be spending more time with her. Next time she asks me to assist on an impromptu photo shoot, I'm in.

And speaking of quality time, Mom tugs at my arm, steering me toward another weekend afternoon of shopping for sporting goods that will surely be wasted on a spazzola like yours truly, but *I don't even mind*. That's how shiny happy sparkly twinkle-some my mood is right this second.

"See you later," I say to Tobin, hoping he's feeling even the smallest fraction of the frenzied, mega-atomic crushage that is coursing through my veins right now. Willing him to do so.

I mean, the mere existence of *Riley Townsend* doesn't, like, *automatically* mean that Tegan is correct, that they're for sure, 169 percent, getting back together, right?

Anytime.

"Definitely," he says.

And all I can do is grin like a fool.

I'm so okay with that.

I float through the rest of the afternoon in a hazy stupor, even going so far as to pretend with Mom that I can tell the difference between one set of ski poles and another (I can't, but I *can* tell that she appreciates the effort).

It's not until much later, back in the warmth of my bedroom, with Ricky Ricardo worrying a hole in the plush shag carpet, that I realize:

My cell phone is missing.

I IM Duncan, since of course texting is out of the question:

Lost my cellie!

He responds immediately:

Oh noes! How ever will u sustain your CIA levels of invading your friends' privacy?

Ha, ha, ha, I type.

Because, I mean, really.

Ha, ha, ha. Indeed.

CHAPTER 10

So,

As it happens, when the sun begins to cease to rise in the mornings, wake-up calls become less a suggestion and more a hard-and-fast system. This is what I learn in early November, four weeks after our arrival, when the Earth shifts on its axis yet again, and the "daylight," such as it is, doesn't break until sometime during the nine A.M's, by which point I'm already off at school and doing my damnedest to care about anything Markman drones on about. Apparently, there's actually something to Dad's biochemistry research, and circadian rhythms and stuff, after all, 'cause I have to deploy a complicated multitier system of alarms just to ensure I manage to drag my butt out of bed every morning.

My saving grace is the cold; even in our custom-weatherproofed house, I swear I feel the air slither through the imperceptible cracks surrounding our tightly shut windows and coil around my ankles in those early, prewake hours where I float, semiconscious, in a quasi-dream state.

There's no getting away from that chill, not with flannel pj's, or wool socks, or even electric blankets.

So I don't bother trying.

Instead, when my windows fog up and my flesh prickles into rigid goose bumps, I go with it. I roll right out from underneath the nest of blankets I build each night, race across my bedroom, and dive immediately into the X-treme-weather wear Mom bought for me.

She wasn't kidding about being into my Traynor phys ed ski session. Apparently, the thought of me outdoors and exercising on a regular basis got her so hyped that in the end I had to question which one of us was more pathetic. I mean, she's the one losing her ever-lovin' mind over insulated snow pants, but then again, I'm the one who's driven her to it. Can't forget that. It's important to own one's personal crazy-pants, I've decided. And I've for sure got mine.

It's ridiculous, my bag of nutterdom—the kind of secret that I really needn't bother keeping to myself; but there's something about *my* mornings, something that I want to hold on to. Speaking of personal crazy: mine is the kind of thing that would rock Mom's world.

I'm telling you: she'd totally pop her gasket if she saw me every morning, before school, before even she or Dad has roused from their bed, rolling silk underwear up along my legs, pulling the drawstring cord on my ski pants so that they lie flat against my hips. Hitching up my mail-order "active outdoor" socks and lacing boots that look like they'd be better suited for scaling Everest than for trotting on down to the center of town, and then trotting right back home again.

Because that's what I do. Every morning, that is. I rise quietly, early, undetected, and dress in the shadows of what should be morning light but is instead a confusing trick of science. I swath myself in layers, feeling shielded, protected, and I head outside.

I walk to town.

I walk to town in the mornings, soaking in the sensation of the air against my cheeks, tactile yet diaphanous, *there*, but only in the negative space that outlines the shape of my body.

Today, *this* morning, when I pause outside of the diner for the moment of clarity that accompanies the faint whiff of bacon grease piping through the building's heating ducts, my eyes focus. They dance over Cady, whom I can see through the window. Her red bouffant do bobs as she weaves from table to table, laying down napkin, fork, knife, napkin, fork, knife, napkin, fork, knife, napkin . . . She pauses, purses her lips, seems to be counting off in her head, then resumes her rhythm. I wonder what it must feel like, to be so sure of one's movements, one's motion. To be so certain of one's forward momentum.

She can't possibly feel my eyes on her. I'm easily five yards away, not to mention, you know, *a plate-glass window separates us*, but still, she looks up, catches my eye. I blush, falter slightly, and begin to retreat. Momentum carries me, blindly, back up the hill and home again.

.ıl

I may be able to dodge my parents, but Chloe, not so much. When I get back to my bedroom, there's an IM window open on my computer screen.

> MissCLOver: Where u been?
> AggghE: Uh, out 4 a walk this a.m. I know, weirdness.
> MissCLOver: Weirdness FO SHO!!! Why would u EVER get up EARLIER THAN ABSOLUTELY NECESSARY?

Chloe is a fan of the excessive use of capitalization in IM conversations. She doesn't mean it in a shout-y way. But still. There is shout-y-ness. I cringe, even all by myself at my computer.

> MissCLOver: But actually was meaning, where u been lately, not this morning-ly. No texts, no

calls, no love from my AggghEEE! What gives?

It's been only a few days since I lost my phone. What with all of the walking and the struggling to keep warm, I guess I haven't had a chance to fill Chloe in. Whoops.

AggghE: OMG 4got 2 tell you that I lost my cell phone! Hence having gone dark. Still haven't replaced it. Hoping will turn up in a bag, or a pocket, or, IDK, under the cushion in RR's bed.
AggghE: (which btw is down-feathered & nicer than MY bed. just sayin'.)

(Because it is. Would that I were joking.)

MissCLOver: RR would notice if it were there, tho. Like the princess and the pea—would bruise his fragile little doggie-derriere. Anyway, s'always the last place you look 4 it . . .
AggghE: Um, that doesn't even make sense.
MissCLOver: Hmm . . . yeah, I guess not. Let's just call it a riddle and move on then . . .
MissCLOver: So, what else? How's Momzer?
AggghE: OK, I guess. Still madly snapping pics of everything in sight, but at least it means she

leaves me alone. I'm telling ya, those Saturday shopping trips were killing me. Not 2 mention—e-spin class. Pics = a big step up!

MissCLOver: Say more. Will there be a Marisol Ramon-Jorges calendar coming out in time for the Xmas season?

AggghE: Ha! That would be amazing. No idea what her plans are for branding & licensing, tho. It started small, dressing up the dog and whatever. But she's all into these "winter landscapes" now. I keep trying to tell her, if u've seen 1 icicle, u've seen 'em all . . .

MissCLOver: Be nice! She's prolly superbored—not 2 mention, FREEZING up there! Brr!

AggghE: Don't take her side! She's totally in my face lately, trying 2 get me 2 "live a little." E-spin class, remember?!

There are some things only your main girl can truly understand.

MissCLOver: Yeah, OK, spin = not the bestest call. But u know ur mom is the cutest & she means well. & she doesn't have any distractions! At least u have school.

AggghE: Yes, school. Joy.

MissCLOver: Institutionalized education has its perks. Like CUTE BOYS.

How does she know these things?

MissCLOver: Really no news with Duncan?

HgyghE: Really really. Friend Zone, I tell ya. FRIEND. ZONE.

MissCLOver: U'r ridic. People can be coaxed out of the FZ, if there's enough lip gloss involved.

AggghE: U know I abstain from glossage on account of how it makes my lips sticky. And it always smells like artificial foodstuffs.

MissCLOver: Ag! AGGGH! U are impossible. But, OK, whatever. So, who else? There's gotta b someone other than Duncan . . .

AggghE: Honestly?

I know Chloe. If I tell her about Tobin, she's just going to encourage me to go for it. A rival like Riley would be no match for Chloe's dogged determination. But I know myself; I'm nothing like Chloe, and that way lies obsession, heartache, and acid reflux.

Still . . .

MissCLOver: Duh. You r pausing = i am right. Spill it.

Chloe knows all. It's no use trying to keep a secret.

AggghE: ::sigh:: There may be a rogue cutie on the horizon. But it's hopeless. He's way outta my league.
MissCLOver: I am so sure, Gorjusness.
AggghE: Pls.
MissCLOver: I swear, I'm buying u one of those daily affirmation journals.
AggghE: R U trying to make me gag?
MissCLOver: Just a fun side effect. 'K, just promise me this: whoever he is, u'll talk 2 him 2day.

I consider the promise. Chloe's heart is in the right place. And anyway, it's an easy one to keep.

AggghE: Well . . . okee. Since u insist.
MissCLOver: Squee! Please IM l8r with all of the gory details.
AggghE: Deal. Here's hoping they're not TOO gory, tho . . . I'm telling you, it's hopeless!

MissCLOver: There's that can-do attitude that I know and love!

.ıll

I pinky e-swear to check in as soon as I have news, and we sign off. I have to admit, it was nice to chat with Chloe, even for a few minutes. It hasn't been so long since I've been cell-phone-less, but I think normal time passes at an accelerated rate between best friends, like the way a regular year is seven years to a dog and stuff.

I shrug on my comfy jeans, slide into my *h*'Uggs, and slip on a fleece over a T-shirt. Not exactly "approaching-Tobin chic," but then again, I don't need to be chic to fulfill my promise to Chloe. Of course I'm going to talk to him today. It'll be painless. Swift. A total no-brainer.

What Chloe doesn't know: it'll also be about as flirty and romantic as a week-old tuna fish sandwich.

We've got gym class today. I'll see Tobin there.

.ıll

"You. Are clearly a natural."

This is what Duncan tells me as I strap my feet into the bindings of my skis.

He is being sarcastic, obvs. We are in phys ed, and we are practicing stepping into our skis, which I had assumed would be the sort of thing that would not require practice.

I had also assumed that it would be the sort of thing that took place outside, on actual snow.

But I assumed incorrectly. On both counts. It turns out that Coach Franklin knows a thing or two about winter sports, and about how much advance preparation it could potentially take a person to learn to step firmly onto two solid fiberglass boards.

You would think—or, at least, *I did* think—that the planes of the skis would anchor me, ground me steadily to the polished wooden floor of the basketball court.

You would think so.

Instead, I feel wildly off balance, as though I'm going to lurch forward at any moment, tilting until my skis are perpendicular to the floor. *That* would be a Mom-worthy Kodak moment, for sure.

Since remaining upright is requiring every last ounce of my energy, I can't be bothered to respond to Duncan's dig. I suck in further, clench my muscles—such as they are—tighter, and tilt my torso just the slightest fraction forward. I reach out, ever-so-light, ever-so-subtle.

And I tap Duncan on the shoulder. Not hard, but

forcefully enough to send him rocking backward.

He's better on skis than I am—like, a *lot* better—but I've caught him off guard. Boy goes down.

He's not hurt, but he looks grumpy and confused. Now his expression is less *knowing* and more *unamused*.

If only he were standing in my place. Then he might be able to see the humor in this situation.

I am unable to suppress a smirk. "You're a natural."

Duncan glares and opens his mouth to say something, but before he can, we hear laughter from over my shoulder. It's laughter I've come to recognize, come to respond to like one of Pavlov's weaker-willed dogs.

Tobin.

He has witnessed my random act of violence, and he seems to find it as chuckle-worthy as I do.

We're *so* totally soul mates, it's not even funny.

"Mockery will get you everywhere," Duncan says, still pretending to be stern.

"Balance is tricky," Tobin replies. And then he winks. He *winks*!

He is speaking to Duncan.

But he is looking at me.

If it weren't for the fact of Riley sidling up behind him, beaming her beatific grin at him, I might even think that Tobin and I were having a Moment.

But who am I kidding? A Moment isn't meant to go three ways.

.ıll

Salvation, I have found, often comes in strange and unexpected ways.

Mine, shockingly, is delivered to me by—of all people— my *father*.

We are at the dinner table that night, the three of us chomping heartily on some Atkins-tastic fish casserole, when he breaks it down.

"I want you to bring some friends to the radio station."

I put down my fork and swallow a bite of sautéed bok choy.

(Side note: Who would have thought that standing stock-still on a pair of skis, indoors, could be so taxing? But it really must have taken it out of me; otherwise, there's no explaining the vigor with which I am attacking this aggressively healthful plate of mushola that passes for dinner tonight.)

"Um," I say. "What?"

"*Qué?*" Mom asks. Her freshly tweezed eyebrows knit together. Guess she didn't get the memo, either.

"Your friends," Dad says again, patient. "From your new

school. Can you gather some of them together and bring them to the station?"

"What for?" I am suspicious. Is this some kind of less-than-subtle attempt to determine whether or not I actually *have* friends? Not cool, Dad. A little faith, please.

"For the show," he says. "I want to do a special segment on SAD and adolescent cognitive function."

Ah. Of course. I should have guessed. *For the show.* There's the rub.

"My friends aren't bummed out," I reply. "They're used to it here." No need to tell him how my "friends" are really mainly Duncan, and that the reason he isn't bummed out is because, unlike me, he's hardly ever bummed out by anything, and certainly not by Alaska. He digs this place the way you would a circus sideshow or a trip to a really cool, exotic location. Which I suppose, to some people, Alaska actually is. (Though not, technically, to someone who was last "new" here back when he still wore training pants. But whatever. Splitting hairs, yada, yada . . .)

"That's exactly the point, Aggie." Dad is starting to sound slightly less patient. "Teens are both more erratic and more resilient. It's a fascinating time in human emotional development."

Well. I am not entirely sure how I feel about being called *erratic,* even *resiliently* or *fascinatingly* so. Hmmph.

But if there's one thing I've become accustomed to over the course of my sadly uneventful life, it's being Dad's own personal case study.

And I guess it does have the occasional perk.

I mean, I can think of at least one "friend" I'd love to invite down to the station. One person I've been dying to find an excuse to talk to, and to spend more time with.

This could actually be completely and totally perfect.

I spear a limp wad of bok choy with renewed spirit. "I have some ideas, Dad," I say, as bright and agreeable as ever.

"Let's make this happen."

.ıl

It is all I can do not to spring from the table and leap up the staircase four steps at a time, so eager am I to flee to my bedroom and get on the horn with someone, anyone, who can bring Tobin Young that much closer to my father's radio show and, likewise, into my immediate orbit. *Riley, Schmiley,* I've got a plan here, people!

Once I've shoveled down as much bok choy as a human being can reasonably ingest in one sitting, I force myself to proceed half tempo, at a normal-person pace, to my bedroom.

It's there, within the privacy of my discarded back issues of *OK!* magazine, that I realize the true folly of my scheme.

I *can't* call anyone.

I *can't*. Call *anyone*. Not one single, solitary person. I can't even dial Chloe in the hopes that she'll give me the pep talk I'll need if I really do plan on reaching out and touching (metaphorically, that is, *le sigh*) He Who Wears His Hair Tousled and Sometimes Smells Like Musk.

(Not that I've taken to, like, surreptitiously *sniffing* Tobin when he passes me by in homeroom, or anything. Swearsies.)

And why not, you ask?

Simple:

My cell phone. It's still missing, obviously.

I've been too nervous to tell my parents that I lost it, and too broke-ous to replace it myself. And also, too much enjoying communicating with Chloe via IM, I suppose, wherein it's easier to shut her out when she's making me fake vow to do things that directly involve stepping outside of my comfort zone, like wearing cheek stain, or attempting small talk with adorable boy-types.

I couldn't possibly have foreseen this moment, after all. This moment is insanity. Madness. Chaos. The very embodiment of an ironic twist. The universe has collapsed in upon itself. I actually *want* to contact a fellow student, a contemporary . . . nay, a *friend* (yes, that's right, Dad, I do actually have a few) . . . but technology has felled me.

Crapola.

But, wait.

Hang on, Aggie . . .

Somewhere in the deepest, most shadowy wrinkles of my brain, a Thought begins to percolate. A Thought that is quickly replaced by a dawning Realization.

Something to do with . . . technology. And . . . my phone. My quasi-genius, high-tech, practically *spy*-tech phone.

My phone, and *its* . . . technology.

Specifically, its GPS system. The same system that allowed me to "pin" Chloe and stargaze from afar can tell me exactly where my pretty little phone is, right down to its precise latitudinal coordinates.

(Not that I'd know what to do with latitudinal coordinates if I had 'em, but *still. STILL.*)

Not so fast, cell phone. Let's talk about this, you and me.

I settle into my desk chair, cackling to myself like a mad scientist. I'm not sure what I'm hoping to accomplish with this little experiment, but something about tracking my cell phone makes me feel more proactive, more . . . *involved.* Even if the only thing I'm involved with, really, is a Google search.

You've gotta start somewhere, right?

I dig inside my topmost desk drawer, fish out the little pamphlets that came with my phone. My cell phone has a serial number, through which I can access it on the manufacturer's Web site.

Genius. *Genius,* I tell you.

A few keystrokes later, my own cell phone number appears onscreen, underscored in blue to indicate that it's a click-through link.

And click through, I do. I totally go for it. There's no holding me back, now.

The little spinning hourglass that tells you when the computer is Thinking whirs and blinks, and I tap my fingers against my desk along with it, restless. I'm not sure why I'm so eager to locate my phone; knowing where it is won't bring me any closer, in the most literal sense of the term, to using it. But there's a curiosity gnawing at the hollow inside my stomach that's as indefinable yet unignorable as my recent proclivities toward Nordic, nomadic walkabout.

(Or, I suppose that bubbly-belly feeling could also be indigestion, but let's not dwell on that.)

And then.

The hourglass stops, and a new box of text appears on my screen. It's an address. *The* address. Of where my phone is. I scan quickly, eager. My space-aged phone matches the address up with its Yellow Pages listing:

Young-Brenner Northern Dogsled Tours.

Huh.

That name sounds awfully familiar.

It takes a minute for me to put two and two together (I never have been much good at math).

And then.

Oh. Oh.

Oh.

No. Effing. Way.

Young-Brenner Northern Dogsled Tours.

YOUNG!

DOGSLED! TOURS!

My cell phone is kickin' it with Tobin Young's father.

This information begs an endless stream of questions. I'll start with this one:

How is it that my *cell phone* is so much closer to the boy of my dreams than I am? Seriously. *How?* Has the God of Unrequited Lurve been at it *again?*

Come on, karma. Riddle me *that.*

CHAPTER 11

It hardly seems fair that my cell phone should have all of the fun.

When you are looking longingly to an inanimate object for life lessons, it's time to reconsider your choices.

I can't let my cell phone have more of a life than I do. I just can't.

Clearly, my only recourse is to take matters into my own hands.

At least I finally have the perfect excuse to track down Tobin, to ask him if he wants to spend time with me in the outside-of-school kind of way.

(And yes, I realize that it isn't exactly date-esque when you and your crush are posing as lab rats for your shrinky-dink dad, but whatevs. Let's not split hairs, here.)

We have a sub for homeroom on Thursday, which basically amounts to anarchy. Good news all around, in that it means I have the perfect opportunity to oh-so-casually talk to Tobin about my father's radio show.

If only it weren't that talking to Tobin is, generally speaking, an anything-but-casual experience for yours truly. I'm so nervous I think my fillings are rattling in the back of my mouth.

(Side note: it's not until you're contemplating approaching the dude of your dreams that you realize how truly crucial dental hygiene is, in the long term. Curse you, fillings!)

I've prepped for my mission as best as I possibly could: went walking this morning, despite the bitter snap to the air, breathing in the green, green, green patchwork expanse and the dusting of powder on the mountains in the distant landscape. Sometimes, Denville feels like a back lot, someplace where adventure movies are filmed.

When I got back from my walk, I was invigorated enough to filch some of my mom's styling crème after washing my hair this morning. I'm still wary of such fancified appliances as the straightening iron, but I think I managed a decent self-blowout, taking into account my relative inexperience in such matters. I even used a "paddle brush," which *Life & Style* insists is the key to a sleek, smooth look.

(Usually, any makeover skills I possess are directed toward Chloe, no matter how much she may try to talk me into embracing the natural wonder known as the "neutral eye palette.")

I am wearing my favorite jeans, the ones with the looser-legged cut, but honestly, I think they're more flattering on my patootie than any of those spandex-y costumes of torture that Mom does heart so. And while I have taken to rocking the *h'*Uggs of late (What can I say? Comfort first), I did dig out a V-neck sweater in a leafy green color that doesn't do horrible things to my chestal region.

I scarfed down a bowl of oatmeal as quickly as I could this morning in an attempt to stave off any potential parental mention of my fashion-forward look, but there is no hiding such things as Juicy Tubes (shade: Desert) from Mom.

"*Mira!*" she exclaimed, looking no less excited and proud than she might if I had, for example, been spontaneously awarded a Nobel Prize. "*Que bonita!*"

"Quit it, Mom," I said, carving valleys into the edge of my oatmeal. "It's no big deal."

Still, I had to admit: for the first time in what felt like forever?

It was kind of nice to be noticed.

It was.

.ıl

"You look different today," Duncan says, squinting at me. "What is it? Did you cut your hair?" He hovers over my desk with an appraising glance that makes me nervous, especially since he's blocking my view of the classroom door, which I've been monitoring like a hawk waiting for Tobin to show up. A hawk with binoculars. On amphetamines.

"No," I say, "just dried it." *Move, Dunc. For the love of all that is good and holy, please, please move.*

"Huh. Works for you," he says. "And, I'm feeling the V-neck. You give good clavicle."

"Thanks." I'm starting to feel warm and uncomfortable. The sweater is cashmere, but it might as well be burlap. I wish Duncan weren't staring at me. Even though he seems to like what he sees.

If only I had actual psychic powers.

He frowns, sending his eyebrows furrowing to a wrinkled point in the center of his forehead. "Are you wearing lip gloss?"

Jeezum. "Yes! Gawd!" I exclaim, straightening in my seat and attempting to look indignant. "Since when is that, like, a crime?" I would probably sound more convincing if my face weren't about to burst into flame.

Boy-scrutiny is stressful.

At this, Duncan cracks, his face breaking into a smile and laughter erupting from his throat. "Oh my god. You're going to go for it again today. You're going to take a stab at social contact with Señor Dreamboat."

I hate that he knows me so well. This is the danger of Friend Zone—you become friends.

I glare at him. "For your information, I am not going to 'go for' anything. I simply have some business to take care of with Tobin, and I thought he might be more receptive to my offer if I were well groomed." No clue as to why I suddenly sound like I've swallowed an executive-themed word-of-the-day calendar

"Are you hitting on him, or selling him a house?"

I swat Duncan with my notebook. "Shut it. I'm offering him the chance to appear on my dad's radio show."

Duncan's eyes widen. "No way!"

"Way. Dad wants some input on depressyitis from 'local teens.'" I make the air quotes with my fingers so as not to be misunderstood.

"I'm in. I'm so in. When do we tape?" Duncan's face is lit up like a Christmas tree.

But now it's my turn to look wary, shiny Duncan Christmas face or no. "Um. Are you sure?" I can't think of a good reason why he shouldn't be, except: Tobin. I was hoping for some alone time with Tobin. And given that Riley is usually stuck to him like Velcro, this may very well be my only opportunity for the foreseeable future.

"Oh, I'm sure. I've got perspective. Not to mention, charisma." He grins at me with a twinkle in his eye, and

I have to admit, there is a definite charismatic vibe going on. Also, he's been obsessed with my dad from day one, and *also* also, he was nice to me on my first day of school, and seems legitimately to enjoy spending time with little old *moi*. Mustn't overlook the kindness of strangers.

And finally, there's the fact that if I do get Tobin to agree to be on the show, I'll want a bud at my side for the whole ordeal. Moral support, strength in numbers, and yada, yada, yada . . .

Unless of course the presence of two boys in such close proximity causes me to faint dead away. Or something even more embarrassing.

"Fine," I say, through gritted teeth, like the decision is killing me. Duncan knows me well enough by now to know when I am kidding. "You're in."

·ıll

Tobin never does show up in homeroom, for reasons that remain a mystery to me and that I hope have nothing whatsoever to do with a random jaunt through the outer wilds of Denville with Riley.

Or with any other girl, for that matter. A random jaunt would put a major crimp in my plans.

Duncan insists on accompanying me to look for him,

which at first sounds like maybe not the best idea, but quickly proves to be brilliant. After all, how better to appear calculatedly casual with Tobin than with another friend at my side while I extend my oh-so-calculatedly-casual invite?

We finally track our dude down in the caf, where he sits, easy, natural, comfortable as ever, dunking crinkle fries into a tiny little paper cup of what I'm going to assume is ketchup.

It is a scientific fact that crinkle fries are one of my very favorite foods. Just another sign that we're so totally meant to be together, if you ask me. That, and the fact that Riley is nowhere to be seen. Success! Bliss! Warm fuzzies!

Duncan spots Tobin at the exact moment that I do, and manages to loop an arm around my hip even while balancing his own lunch tray against his torso. What would it be like, I wonder, to be graceful, self-assured? To be unself-conscious enough to court the God of Embarrassing Clothing Stains so wantonly by pressing a tray of foodstuff against one's person?

I may never find out. And so be it. I follow Duncan across the crowded room.

Tobin is sitting with a few other crunchies whom I recognize as his buds from the ski team. I think one's named Mitch, and one might be Kurt. Strong, sturdy one-syllable names to match their strong, sturdy athletic frames. Or,

Kurt might actually be called Adam. But for now they'll all just be "hey," to me.

"Hey." Duncan leans in before I have a chance to, resting his tray against the edge of Tobin's table.

Tobin looks up, his usual wide smile breaking across his face. "Hey, guys, what's up?" he asks. "Wanna sit?" He looks to either side of himself. "I think we can squeeze."

We can squeeze. I mean, really: it's adorable that he's truly the Nicest. Guy. Ever. But come now: no amount of squeezing is going to fit my backside at that full-up table, even if I were to take to walking from here to the southernmost point of Florida every single day from now until my last dying breath.

I say, "It's okay." I swallow. "We just, I mean— I just -"

"We're here about your fifteen minutes of fame," Duncan bursts in, practically gushing, he's so excited.

For his part, Tobin looks extremely confused. I don't blame him.

"My dad," I say, as though those two words offer any sort of clarity whatsoever. For obvious reasons, Tobin's face registers no further understanding. I try again. "He wanted me to get together some of the kids from Traynor to be interviewed on his radio show, and so . . . uh . . . I thought of you."

I thought of you. Classic understatement. As though

I don't spend half of my waking hours thinking of Tobin independent of anything my dad may or may not have requested of me. But better not to mention that. There is such a thing as playing it cool, after all.

(Or so I'm told.)

Tobin looks curious, if a little bit uncertain. "I mean, I don't know anything about radio," he begins.

"You wouldn't need to," I assure him, relieved to have something concrete to say at last. "I don't know if you've heard his show, but he does studies on depression, and daylight, and exposure to sunlight, and stuff. It's why we're here. In Alaska, I mean."

Oh, yeah. Way to play it cool, Ag.

"I know," Tobin says, and the idea that he knows even that much about me nearly derails me once and for all. I almost cannot think about anything else, much less continue on with my little rehearsed-speech invite, until Duncan jabs me in the ribs with a not-so-subtle prod to NOT BLOW THIS.

"He wants a teenager's perspective," I finish. "He'd just ask you some questions. It's totally casual. And it's not live, so if you, like, flub anything, it can be edited later."

Just in case you spazz out thoroughly, the way I always do when I'm within thirty feet of you, my lovely. I mean, you never know.

"That I can handle," Tobin says. "As long as you swear I don't need to be some kind of expert."

"Totally not." *Unless you want to be the expert at kissing me . . .*

Duncan jabs me again. "It'll be fun," I conclude. Because listening to Tobin read aloud from my physics textbook would be fun. And also: he smells like musk again today. It's making me slightly dizzy.

Everything is falling into place, like a puzzle or the colored shards of a kaleidoscope just as they begin to form something abstract and gorgeous, multifaceted. Everything is dazzle-y and perfect and shining.

And then.

The dazzling thing takes form, and that form is a lithe, slender shape. A Riley shape. Gah! Where did she come from? How did she know? Does she have some kind of Tobin LoJack chip implanted in her brain?

Riley places her slender, delicate hand on Tobin's forearm. It's so dainty and feminine it could be an ad for nail polish or something.

I want to swat it away. Is there a way to do that without giving myself up as a complete psychopath?

Probably not.

"It'll be so fun," Riley chimes in, beaming, her skin naturally flushed, tinged with a shade most ordinary humans can achieve only through judicious use of Chloe's beloved cheek stain. "Ohmigod, that's so cool of you to ask us."

Us. That's so cool of you to ask *us.*

A squeak of protest forms at the back of my throat, but I force it down. It was never going to be just the two of us, just Tobin and me, anyway. And besides, could it really be "alone time" when you're being taped for a syndicated satellite audience?

Anyway, Dad asked me to bring "friends," plural, and even if I'm stretching it to refer to this group as my posse, I know Papi will be happy.

So, "us" it is, then. Meaning: Tobin, and Duncan, and Riley, and—heck—probably Tegan, and Mitch, and maybe even Kurt/Adam, too.

Yeah, Dad'll be happy. For sure.

Which, I mean: that makes one of us.

CHAPTER 12

Yesterday, my cell phone was

on a bird-watching tour. It seems we're all trying new things of late.

I'm not gonna lie: it's times like these that I *really* miss Chloe.

Specifically, I miss her when all available surfaces in my bedroom are covered with clothing, every article of which screams, "Boring," "Blah," or, even worse, "You only *think* your butt looks less huge in those! [Insert evil-laughter sounds HERE] . . ."

Such times as these don't happen often, but when they do, they quickly escalate to code-magenta proportions. And then, I really, really, *really* miss Chloe.

This afternoon is the radio-show taping. And don't get me wrong: I contemplated Skyping Chloe and modeling different outfits for her, but the thought was too depressing to bear.

(I mean, don't they say that the camera adds ten pounds?

Who needs it? Not to mention, I *also* don't need Chloe freaking out about how I'm going to be seeing Tobin *outside of school*, because, believe you me, I'm freaking out quite enough about it all on my own, thankyouverymuch. She'd just be all, "Go for it!" and "Rah-rah!" and encouraging and stuff, and I am sorry to say that I am just not as adventurous as my cell phone.)

So instead of Skype, I tore like a whirling dervish through my closet, tossing shirts, sweaters, and jeans in every direction. I mixed and matched combos the way you might with a kiddie flip book, or a set of Barbie dolls.

But in the end, the truth of the matter is, I just don't have a very exciting wardrobe. Certainly nothing that screams, "Love me, Tundra God, Tobin! Lay your flannel-clad arms on my bod!"

(And, yeah, I know Duncan said he was all down with my clavicle and stuff, but I just wore that green V-neck the other day, when I tried to dress "up" to invite Tobin to the radio show in the first place. That V-neck may have been it for Vaguely Sexy-ish Separates Owned by Aggie.)

I can't believe my lack of foresight! I can't, can't, *can't* believe my own crappy nonplanning.

That V-neck was, like, my last great hope of being at all cute. What was I *thinking*? (Other than wanting to be Vaguely Sexy for talking to Tobin, that is . . .)

I have to leave for the show in *127 minutes*—barely enough time to master this odd instrument known as the eyelash curler, which *Star* promises me will boost my lashes to Kardashian levels—and there is no solution to my crisis in sight.

(As if I don't have enough to worry about, without adding my eyelashes to the mix. Eyelashes were one of those body parts that I hadn't realized could really be improved upon.)

These are desperate, desperate times, indeed.

I sigh, and shove aside a rejected peach-colored thermal top and brown cords (because: *earth tones much, Ags?*) so that I can sit down at my computer and, with any luck, distract myself for at least a second or two.

My fingers know what I'm up to even before my brain does.

They fly across the keyboard, my DIY raisin-colored manicure (I'm told anything in the wine family is a very "winter" shade) creating a pleasantly blurred aura. And there it is, in black-and-white (well, and yellow, too, thanks to some flash animation, but who's keeping score?):

My cell phone's latest adventure.

I don't know where I was expecting to find my cell phone since the last time I logged on, when it was hangin' at the aviary. I guess I figured that maybe cell phones need downtime, too.

Not mine, though. No way, *Jose*. My cell phone is totally hard-core.

As a matter of fact, my cell phone has totally outgrown such small-time mom-and-pop ventures as Young-Brenner Dogsled, and has moved on to bigger and better things. Things like: Bob's Guaranteed Wildlife Viewing Tours.

(And, while we're on the topic, side note: What's the guarantee there, Bobby? Are you guaranteeing the viewing of wildlife? The functionality of your touring vehicles? The return of participants safely back into the arms of their loved ones? It's all very unclear. A guarantee needs a little more specificity in order really to *mean* anything, I should think.)

But, so. Yeah. My cell phone.

It's quite the Arctic explorer, it is.

I'm completely fascinated by my cell phone's epic journey, never mind perplexed about its transport from point A to point B to point Wildlife Viewing. Someone has found it, of course. Adopted it as his or her own, incorporated it into an aggressively active lifestyle.

(Perhaps an Olympian? Or a retired cartographer? Or—oh, oh!—I'm guessing someone who knows a little something about *swashbuckling*! A swashbuckler. Yes! That *must* be it.)

I suppose I should be worried, concerned about this anonymous, faceless person who has absconded with my phone. Presumably, he or she is also *using* it, running up a bill that dear old Dad pays for.

But here's the thing: the phone plan, I know, is one of those umbrella, family dealies. And it's covered by the radio station. And the coverage kicks butt because of how we're transplants, with roots back home, and people, friends, and family to keep in touch with. So, whatever. Maybe in a week or two, my curiosity will subside, the novelty will wear off, and I'll track down the phone, or let my dad know to cancel the account.

Heck, maybe I'll need to call someone and will *need* to get my hands on a new cellie.

But for now, I'm merely awestruck by my cell phone and its new partner in crime. This imaginary person of unfathomably limitless energy, who is exactly the opposite of all of the things that I am.

I bet this person would have exactly the right outfit to wear to the taping of a satellite-radio-show interview, with her soul mate and several other random hangers-on.

Stupid person. Stupid brave, outgoing person. Stupid person who is so, so, *so* not me.

My cell phone, too, has guts these days. Ever since it managed to shake *me*. These days, my cell phone is living large. My cell phone has personality. My cell phone would not be felled by this small hitch in my life plan.

Huh.

I swivel in my desk chair, survey the fashion wreckage that litters my bed. Here's a question, and it's not a hypothetical. I seriously want to know, folks:

If it were somehow in my position (which, given the powers it's recently demonstrated, might not be so implausible)—

What Would My Cell Phone *Wear*?

What Would My Cell Phone *Do*?

And why can't I figure it out—and *do* it, whatever *it* may be—*myself*?

.ıll

Sometimes it helps to have a meddlesome mother, a mother with *absolutemente* no respect for personal boundaries.

That is to say, sometimes it helps to have a mother like mine.

I'm not sure how she knows, how she puts her pert, dainty finger on the precise moment that I teeter on the brink of a full-on, large-scale, comprehensive meltdown. But she does.

Thirty minutes after realizing that my cell phone has bigger *cojones* than I do, I hear a rap at my bedroom door. We still have almost two hours before we have to leave for the studio, but that's about three days, five hours, and forty-five minutes fewer than I would reasonably need to get myself together and get out the door looking vaguely presentable.

"Yeah." I could be friendlier. But I'm not. I'm all tapped out of friendly. Which sucks, considering I'm supposed to be spending the day with some *friends*. Even if most of them are more like just acquaintances . . .

"I can come in?"

"You can come in." I have to admit, I'm intrigued. It's not often that Mom sounds tentative.

The door swings open, and Mom steps into my room. My eyes pass over her and widen. She's like the virgin mother (if I believed in that sort of thing). Somewhere, a choir of angels has just begun to chant.

From the doorway, my mother holds out a sweater dress.

It's perfect—cable-knit, with a crew neck and three-quarter sleeves, in a heathered charcoal knit. It's totally casual, but totally cute. It'll actually look good on my squareish frame. It'll go with the *h'*Uggs so I don't look like I'm trying too hard.

It's perfect, perfect, perfect.

How? How did she know?

She is like a psychic clothing fairy. A fairy godmother, and I am the fairy-tale princess awaiting transformation. Amazing. I am amazed.

I must be grinning at her like a loon, because she smiles

back at me, a pleased sort of knowing etched across her face. "You like it?" As if it weren't obvious.

"It's *perfect*." I can't seem to find another word. It's such a simple thing, the dress—you would probably pass it by in the store and not think anything of it—but it's 138 percent ideal for my purposes, my body, my personality.

Now, I have something to wear. I have the *best* thing to wear. Now, I won't have to kill myself. I can go to the studio and do the interview like originally planned. Which will be *so* much more fun than throwing myself off of a bridge and stuff . . .

She moves toward me, holding the dress out. "*Mira,* put it on so we can do the makeup."

Hold up, now.

The record skips abruptly, plunging the sound track in my head into silence.

Sweater-dress fever is one thing, but Mom's version of "doing the makeup" might be a step further than I'm willing to go right now.

(I mean, the woman is a former soap star, ya know? I'm sure you can appreciate my apprehensions.)

"It's fine. I'll be fine." I jump up and quickly begin to shimmy into the dress, ready to lock myself in the bathroom if she decides to come at me with a pair of tweezers.

She purses her lips, watching me wrestle a pair of leggings

into submission (it's true, I have gone over to the dark side, embraced the leggings. What can I say? They're comfy. And ever since I've been walking in the mornings, it's almost like I have leg muscles and stuff!).

"Is not 'fine.' You need the makeup to look good for the camera when I take my *fotografías*."

"Come, on, Mom, just leave it," I say. I face myself in the mirror, smooth the wool over my belly so that there's no pooch.

It occurs to me: gray may not be my best color. I mean, sure, it's a classic, a neutral, you can't really go wrong, but the fact is that the green sweater from the other day did more for the teeny-tiny flecks of gold in my eyes. Not like I need this dress in candy-apple red or anything like that—let's not go crazy now, people—but, like, a soft powder blue could be pretty. You know? My mom may do everything in her earthly power to modify and manipulate what the God of Good Genes gave her, but the truth is, my plain old, untouched, no-frills genes aren't the worst in the whole entire world, either. I look like a rounder, fuller, paler version of my mother: dusty brown hair that's wavy and completely unprocessed, brown eyes that apparently pick up a glint of gold when I dare to embrace color. Cheeks that are more pink than California Sunless Spray orange.

It's possible I'm even . . . dare I say it . . . a little bit . . . *cute?*

Just as it dawns on me how un-Aggie it is to be contemplating wearing something other than basic black, white, or denim—to be considering my own cuteness—the relativity of, the meaning of what Mom's just said hits me in full.

I spin to face her. "Wait," I say, panic rising in my voice. "You're coming?" And then, a moment later, upon further refection— "*Wait.*"

This time there is no mistaking my dismay.

"*You're taking pictures?*"

.ıll

Click!

"*Mira, chicos, say queso!*"

Click!

It's 3:09 P.M. The interview begins taping in six minutes.

There's still time to jump off that bridge, I think. *All you need is a little motivation. Where's that can-do cell-phone spirit?*

"Cheese!" Of course Duncan sings it proudly, the one long, drawn-out syllable reverberating with power as he projects from the diaphragm.

Click!

We're all in the studio now, Tobin, Duncan, Tegan, Kurt/ Adam, Riley, and me. And—oh, yes—Mom and Ricky Ricardo, too.

(In the thank-jeezum-for-small-favors category, Ricky is wearing a simple black T-shirt. Mom thinks it's "arty." So that's something. It could definitely have been *way* worse. There could have been a beret involved, *por ejemplo* . . .)

Per Mom's little last-minute bombshell, she's here chronicling the whole event on film (or, er, on jpeg, really, but same diff, right?). She's convinced the *Miami Herald* will want an exclusive on these images, or if not, "I can post them on my weblog, *sí?*"

Her *weblog*. She has a *weblog* devoted to her photography. Horrors. I shudder even to contemplate.

"Sounds perf, Mrs. E," Duncan chimes in, still beaming and mugging like some kind of supermodel. He gets a major kick out of my mother, thinks she's "a trip." Easy for him to say—she's not *his* mother, you know? All I can say is, if this is a trip, I want my return ticket. *Stat.* And I don't want to think about what Tobin must be making of this whole scene.

He's *acting* very non-nonplussed, I have to say, smiling mildly and letting his gaze run the length of the studio interior. He's acting like he thinks that being here is maybe-kinda-sorta cool. And it definitely doesn't hurt that Tegan and Riley have been cooing ever since they first walked through the door.

The funny thing about this all is that, like I say, Dad's show isn't live. So we feel very official and fancy sitting in the studio with our oversized headphones on, leaning toward control panels that look like they control spacecrafts, not microphones, and taking note of the bazillions of blinking lights everywhere, but the truth is that if Duncan wanted to spend the next forty minutes making farting sounds with his armpits, he could, and we could tape it, and edit it, and *no one would ever have to know.*

(Not that I think that's what he's planning on doing. Armpit farts seem like a very un-Duncan thing, most definitely. I'm just saying: everything gets cleaned up in the editing.)

Anyway, we're all lined up in a row with our scripts that I printed out for us last night. We're supposed to answer Dad's questions naturally, but he still wanted us to be prepared. And even today, we spent a few minutes going over what exactly would go down once taping started in earnest.

Mom and Ricky have to stay outside of the recording studio, on account of spontaneous, uncontrollable animal spazz-outs, and random fits of bark-sneeze combos. Mom is still snapping away with the *fotografías*, though: she apparently has some special Photoshop-y tool on her

MacBook that can remove the glare of the glass pane between us from her finished product.

For her *weblog*.

"Everybody ready?" Dad asks jovially, and I can't help it: there's a little hiccup in my stomach that says even though I'm way too old, and I've been dealing with my dad and his fake-fancy job for so, so long now, I'm still the eensiest bit nervous. I don't know why that is, and I don't know what to do about it. So I just swallow it down as best I can.

Duncan reaches over, squeezes my knee. Smiles at me. He's not nervous at all, I can tell. I don't know how or why, but he's been, like, waiting his whole entire life for someone to shove a microphone under his nose and ask him what he thinks. About anything.

How are some people like that?

I breathe in deeply, hoping that maybe the air around him is somehow charged, that it will maybe relax me. Will reconfigure my DNA into whatever insane arrangement keeps Dunc so perma-clean, cool, and minty-fresh.

Tegan giggles, and even Riley lets out a little squeal.

"*So* ready," Riley says. She sounds like I do when I'm trying to fake confidence, except with her it's so totally not fake.

For the record, though: she's wearing jeans, not a dress, but still, her top is clingy and ruffled and there's something flippy happening to the ends of her hair. It doesn't look the way it usually does in school.

I'm not the only one who gave thought to her appearance today.

Somehow, that's the key—that's the realization that sends a shot of Zen directly into my bloodstream. *Riley is human, too.* Riley spends time on her hair. Riley looked in the mirror this very morning and thought, *I would like to do something slightly special. Something slightly different than what I usually do. Something about today matters to me.* Even knowing that we're going to be on the radio, where people can't even see us.

So that's something that we have in common, Riley and I. Something *other* than the fact that we both seem to swoon whenever we get within four feet of the Tobinator, I mean.

I sneak another sideways glance at her, leaning forward in my folding chair so that I can see past Duncan's profile. She wears tiny silver drop earrings, delicate sand dollars in a hammered metal that glint when she turns her head from side to side. I wonder if they're, like, her lucky earrings, or something. Or if they're what she wears when she's trying to look like she isn't *trying* to look like anything. Or if maybe her mother came into her room this morning and gave them to her, special for today, a surprise, a present, and said, "I thought you might want these."

I turn my head and see my mother smiling away on the other side of the window that separates the sound booth from the rest of the studio. She flashes me a subtle thumbs-up beneath everyone else's sight line. I nod an acknowledgment as coolly as I can.

She raises her camera once more, aims it at me. This time, I don't flinch, or roll my eyes, or turn away. This time, I meet the lens with a steady gaze. And though the walls of our booth are obviously soundproof, I swear, I hear the mechanical *click* as it triggers again.

I think, *Cheese.*

And offer up a small, secret smile to my mother.

···ıl

Obviously, this moment isn't to last.

Whatever that happy wholesomeness was that passed between Mom and me goes right out the window the second that taping starts. Once taping starts, Mom immediately launches into a parody of what you might think a professional photographer does—crouching, leaping, nodding to herself, and all the while snapping away. It's frenetic, frenzied. And extremely embarrassing. Duncan keeps a hand on my elbow throughout, trying to steady me, aware that I'm one electronic click away from a full-on meltdown.

Luckily, Riley and Tobin are way too involved in making googly eyes at each other to take too much notice of my mother. It's these questions that I prepared for Dad. My mistake was in leading the witnesses. But how could I have known? How could I have possibly foreseen that a query as innocent as "What's life in a small town *really* like" would have such disastrous consequences?

My stomach clenches just thinking about it. The way that Riley smiled shyly, crookedly, and said, "Well, the thing is that, no matter what happens, we all grew up together. We all have . . . *history* together."

She stole a glance at Tobin that was loaded with meaning, and I swallowed back the bile rising at the back of my throat.

Tobin flushed, looking awkward, and for a moment I thought he wasn't thrilled with the sudden side trip down Memory Lane. But Riley wasn't finished.

"Tobin and I, we went to Homecoming when we were freshmen," she offers. "It was our first big high school dance. And, um, you know, whether we're still together or not"—she at least had the decency to look vaguely abashed as she forced those words out—"we'll always be connected in a special way."

To my utter horror, Tobin nodded. He reached out and put his hand on Riley's knee. And a small fist of disappointment settled in the base of my stomach.

This was a stupid idea. Radio shows are stupid. And Tegan, who is watching me watch Riley and Tobin like the cat that ate the canary, is perhaps the stupidest of all.

Dad yells, "Cut" (no, I'm serious—he really does, like he thinks he's Tarantino or something), and we all slide our headphones off and glance at one another nervously, like maybe one of us accidentally has our fly down, or food on our face, or something else sort of intimate and embarrassing. I don't know why. It's not like anyone revealed anything all that weird or personal during the interview—other than Riley's pathetic display, that is—but there's this collective sense that we've shared something, and it's . . . well, it's awkward, and a little bit unsettling.

It *definitely* doesn't help that Tegan's still playing "What's that smell?" I've just come to accept that expression as her default face.

Everyone kind of shifts in their seat, and then Tobin breaks the bizarro spell with a shrug. "That was cool." He stands up, stretches, and for a second I can see a thin band of exposed skin as his shirt rides up his chest. I literally have to force myself to look away before fainting dead to the ground.

"Thanks for having us, Dr. . . ." Now he trails off, and I can tell he's wondering just how comfortable he's allowed to be, here. Again with the awkward unsettlement. I'm sensing a theme, here.

"Dr. Bob is fine," my dad offers.

Fine. I love it. Like he doesn't *live* for that crap. *Fine.* Please. Can I just say: understatement?

Click.

We all filter out into the main area of the studio, everyone gravitating toward their respective stuff while Mom still makes like a shutterbug. Ricky Ricardo yaps and jumps up and down like he hasn't seen us in forty-seven years, instead of just forty-seven minutes, like he totally forgot that human beings other than my mom even exist and he can't contain his joyousness. The noise makes me thoroughly *loca*, but Riley just laughs and leans down to pat him, falling backward on her butt completely as he scampers into her lap and pelts her with doggie kisses that are seriously verging on PG-13.

"He likes you," Mom says, ever observant. She *finally* lays the camera down on a side table.

"Ohmigod, all animals love Riley, seriously," Tegan chimes in.

Because: of *course* they do. Because Riley is a friend to all creatures great and small. I mean, you knew that, right? Or, at least, you could see it coming?

Riley is such a cliché. In the best and worst possible way, I mean.

Really it's a good thing that, ultimately, Tobin would never, ever go for me. Seriously. Because if there were even the slightest glimmer of a chance that it could happen? And my deepest suspicions were, in fact, correct, and Riley was my competition for his, if not *love,* then at least his hot-and-heavy-ish *like*? Yeah—in that little hypothetical scenario, I wouldn't stand a chance.

So, you know, silver lining and all that re: his apparent *total lack of interest* in *moi.*

(It's important to stay positive.)

And of course, I'm not the only one who thinks he's completely and totally adorbs. Riley may have won points with the Mom on Ricky Ricardo's recommendation, but Mom has been foaming at the mouth to get chatty with Tobin ever since he talked to Dad about his own father's dogsled tour business.

She knew about it, of course, from meeting his mom at the gym, and bumping into him in town that time. But *holy tortilla,* was she ever keen to learn about the fine print. When Tobin described his father's business, she went utterly cuckoo. I should have predicted her reaction. In the moment, I knew it. In that very instant when the subject came up, I looked at her through the studio window and could see the pinpoint-precise, determined glint in her eyes.

I *knew* she was going to go ape over this.

And I've been dreading the point that we would all step out of the studio and directly into her line of special, soap-y, high-drama, industrial-strength *fuego*. Dreading it ever since Tobin's big reveal.

Mom doesn't disappoint. Hence my bracing, my bristling, which stiffens my spine and sets my teeth on edge.

Exhibit A:

"*Miirrraa* Tobin!" she trills now, rolling her *r*'s like Carmen Miranda on Ecstasy. "I loved learning more about your father's business. It sounds *muy interesante*."

I groan. *Here we go.* I would gladly trade the sweater dress for a mother who knows how to dial it down when there's cuteness on the premises. But my mom's dial broke many years ago. In fact, she may have actually been born without an Off switch.

Tobin looks, as any rational, sane person might, slightly unnerved by her enthusiasm, which can only be described as "clinical." To his credit, though, he keeps his composure. Less so Duncan, who, from over Tobin's shoulder, is shooting me *Oh-Lord-WHAT-NOW?* eyes. I blink furiously at him, hoping he'll understand that it is about to *go down,* and that there's nothing that either of us can do about it. It's when you brace for the fall that you fracture the worst. It's better just to go limp and absorb the shock.

"Yeah, he's been doing it for a while, now," Tobin says. "It's pretty corny, I guess, but the tourists really like it. And, you know, I think of all the tours out there, his is really one of the best, for the price and stuff." He reddens, thrusting his hands into his pockets. "I sound like an ad or something."

"No, no, no," Mom says, even though—*yes, yes, yes (but SO WHAT?)*—he kind of does. "Is sweet. I wish Aggie would be so excited about what her father and I do. I think she's secretly embarrassed by my job."

Secretly embarrassed by her job? *Secretly?*

Okay.

There's nothing secret about my shame. A mother who is a telenovela actress is one of the more major checks in the freak-show column that a girl can have to deal with.

And.

"Mom. You don't have a job. You quit, remember?" There's another one of those record-skip moments, and this one, I know, is not just in my head. Though I'm only speaking the truth, my words do sound a little flat, even to my own ears. Harsh, hollow.

Duncan raises his eyebrows at me. *Don't be a blitch*, is what those eyebrows say. *Even though you kind of already were.*

Mom waves her hand. "Yes, from the *televisio*, I retired. It is the truth. But I mean that you are not excited about my photographing. You make fun of my weblog."

Is she *trying* to crawl underneath my skin? I don't think I can handle Mom weirdness in the same confined space as Tobin hotness. I just don't have that kind of strength of character. I am not a person of great moral fortitude, you know?

"Mom! I didn't even know you *had* a 'weblog' until today!" Come to think of it, I guess I've just been taking it for granted that she hasn't been in my face quite so much lately.

Huh.

But anyway. I'm trying—and failing—to keep my cool. I can't believe we're having this . . . this . . . well, not quite *argument*, but whatever it is, in front of everyone. How could the same person who styled me from head to toe for this afternoon be striving so thoroughly to unravel her own work? Grr.

She turns to Tobin as though I haven't even spoken, as though I'm nothing more than a flea dangling from Ricky Ricardo's Swarovski-studded collar. "You don't make fun of your *padre*, Tobin, yes?"

"Yes," he says, looking at me with an almost guilty expression on his face. "I mean—no. I don't make fun of him. I guess not," he stammers.

Mom's face registers triumph, like she has proven something epic through this admission she's garnered from Tobin. For his part, Tobin looks guilty and a wee bit uneasy.

"I'm sure Aggie will not like it," she says, which is *not*

an auspicious beginning to any proclamation, "but I would love to come and take the pictures of your father's tour!"

Bridges, I think again, feverishly. *We need bridges to jump off of.*

"I'll be there after school on Wednesday," Tobin says, glancing at me. I look away. "If you want, I can give you a tour then."

First my cell phone, then my mother—everyone gets closer to my crush than I do.

"The only thing is, it will be dark. If you're going to come in the afternoon, it will be dark." Tobin looks worried, as though a little darkness could ever deter my mother. Please. She's practically a one-woman glowworm.

Mom shrugs, beaming. "*Es no problemo,*" she assures him. "I can bring a flash."

CHAPTER 13

"Eat something. You need to keep your strength up. We can't have you wasting away." Duncan pushes a plate of cheese fries toward me.

As soon as we broke free of the radio-show taping, he practically tossed me over his shoulder and shoved me into his car, making a beeline for the diner. "You need to cool down," he told me, gesturing for me to unzip my window even though it's, like, subzero temps outside today. With the advent of winter, the sky has turned a dreary shade of perma-gray that tinges the tips of the distant mountains a cloudy blue. They are the color of the inside of my brain, I decide: cloudy and blue.

I arch an eyebrow at Duncan—we both know there's no danger of my wasting away anytime soon—but pick at the plate of greasy goodness as instructed. Normally, I'd be all over the comfort-food thing, but for some reason, today, this limp pile of salt and fat just isn't doing it for me. Truly, wonders never will cease.

"Doesn't she *know*?" I moan, for what has to be the seventh time in about as many minutes. "Doesn't she get how totally humiliating it is for her to be clinging to the boy I'm lusting after? I mean, it's just wrong on so many levels."

Duncan makes a sympathetic noise. "Your mom's a special case, I'll grant you that," he concedes. "But I don't think she means to do it. Like, I don't think her actual intended purpose is to embarrass you."

This does nothing to comfort me. "Who cares, though? If the end result is the same, I mean?" I know Mom's "flirt voice" isn't even something she has any control over. I know she was genuinely *that* excited to meet Tobin's father and make with the snappity-snap, but . . . who cares? Honestly, who?

"Put yourself in her shoes," Duncan says. "You've got school, stuff to keep you busy. What has she got here in Alaska, other than her *weblog*?" He chuckles to himself.

I'm in no mood for chuckling. "Don't take her side." I glare at him and flatten a cheese fry beneath the tines of my fork. That's how I feel: flattened.

"I'm not taking sides. It's totally lame that she gets all hyper around the boy you're jonesing for, no doubt. But I don't think it helps you to get all bent out of shape about it. You're not gonna change her."

"You sound like my father, you know?" This is not a

compliment. "And anyway, you should be talking to her. *She's* the one who wishes she could change *me*. Make me pretty and perfect and perky, like she is."

As if. As if that were ever, had ever been, a real possibility.

"Aggie." Duncan gives me a *seriously?* face. He ticks off on his fingers, like a checklist, as he speaks. "One: you *are* pretty. Two: I hate perky. And three: no one is perfect."

I push aside for the moment the belly tingle that comes from Duncan calling me pretty. "Some people are," I mumble, looking down at the potato mush on my plate. "Perfect, I mean. My imaginary sister was."

I pick up my fork again. *Mush, mush, mush.*

That's it, really: the reason I know that, no matter what, no matter how, I will never, ever live up to my mother's expectations.

You can't compete with a ghost. Trust me, I've tried.

Duncan hasn't caught on to the delicate shift in my mood. He's still chuckling, though he's trying to pull himself together.

"Is that anything like an imaginary friend?" he asks. "'Cause, honey, you're supposed to let those go after kindergarten."

"Not *imaginary*," I correct myself. "More like, almost." My voice catches on the word *almost*, and Duncan prickles, snaps to attention, realizing.

I pause, take a breath.

Suddenly, the smell from the fries is cloying, like a heavy film that flips my insides over. I push the plate off to the side of our table. I look at Duncan, really *look* at him to see that he is listening to me. Because what I am about to say is a little bit important. It's something I don't talk about too much.

"I was supposed to have a sister."

"What?" Duncan speaks softly, like he knows that if he pushes too hard, this moment will crack like an eggshell. Now he gets it.

"Well, that was the plan, anyway. My parents, they wanted another kid. A girl."

Really, they wanted another me. I wasn't enough. That was clear right from the start.

But.

Duncan waits. Doesn't prod, barely breathes. Knows that there is more to come.

"My mom tried and tried. She got pregnant, once. But she lost it, like, really early on."

Duncan nods but doesn't say anything. The moment stays, balanced, suspended between us, sticky and fragile like a spiderweb.

"And I guess that happens a lot, or more than you'd think, anyway, but for whatever reason, they told her she shouldn't get pregnant again."

There were theories, hushed conversations that I became aware of only once I was older, mainly having to do with my mom's low body weight, the way that she'd starved herself back when she was still modeling and competing in pageants. Even when she was pregnant with me, she was supercareful about her body. She likes to brag about how she put on only twenty pounds the whole time she was carrying me.

Is it any wonder I've been stuffing my face ever since I popped out of the womb? I was born starving, people. I've been trying to make up for it ever since.

Much to Mom's dismay.

"Wow." It's one syllable, but it tells me that Duncan knows, intuitively, how much pressure that must be. To be the one who made it, the one who's here. The one shot at perfection.

"Yeah."

I tell him about all of it, all of the parts I know, at least: how Mom had it all planned out. Everything about my existence was pristine, placed just so: my bedroom, my clothing, my Gymboree calendar. My mother had an idealized version of a daughter in her head, and with just the one chance to get it right . . . well . . .

She had just set herself up for disappointment. Even back then, the way she tells it, I'd screech and twist and holler if she tried to do me up in happy, shiny pink barrettes and other girly things.

Even then, I existed in opposition to my mother. Despite her best efforts. Or maybe, because of them.

Once I was old enough for preschool, Mom went back to work. Motherhood had apparently given her what my father tactfully termed "easier access to her emotions," and she wanted to use it. She wanted to act. It didn't take long for her to find work on her soap. She had the body for the diva ingenue role; that was for sure.

Well. We all know how that story turned out.

It's not a very long story, only twelve years or so, but it's the full history of why I stick to neutral shades, why I prefer to serve as backup for the folks with the full-on personality. It's the story of why there's no possible way to live up to my mother's image of what a daughter should be. It's the story of why it can be harder, sometimes, to be the one who's here than the alternative.

Because, I *know*. I know what she sees.

When my mother looks at me, really takes me in from head to toe, I know exactly what runs through her mind. I know she notes the ten extra pounds, the baggy jeans, the charcoal tones, the tendency to self-sideline. The idea that I am the chorus girl in someone else's solo Broadway finale.

I know she thinks these things. I *know*. And I know she

thinks about how different it could have been. How different *I* could have been.

If I'd been someone different.

If I'd been a perfect, pristine, shiny pink princess.

Yeah, right.

If I'd been anyone other than me.

···

The best thing about Duncan, if there is one thing that really is the best, is that he doesn't say a word while I'm talking. He doesn't make any weird faces or even those little sympathetic clucks and sighs that people sometimes throw in to show how much, how hard they're truly *listening* to you. After that one simple "wow" escapes from his lips, he settles back, open and awake, taking in the messy spill of emotions that pour from me like a burst faucet. He's like a sponge, squishy and comfortable and there, in that moment, for the sole purpose of catching my runoff.

It makes me wonder how it is that I never talked about this with anyone, ever, before. But of course, that's just Duncan. He's not anyone. He's one good thing about coming to Alaska, I decide. One really good thing that I couldn't have found anywhere else in the world. I may not love living here. But I'm not so dumb that I take this for granted. Someone like Duncan—a *friend* like Duncan—could be worth the effort. Could even be worth the inconvenience of—

Waitaminute.

I sit up, disbelieving. "Is that *snow*?"

Duncan straightens, turns toward the window. Fat flakes touch lightly to the ground. They melt immediately upon contact, but there's no denying it: it's totally snowing.

"Crap," Duncan says, startling me. "I don't have a brush for the windshield."

Right. The windshield. From inside the diner, it's easy to see the crystal downfall as something magical, beautiful, transformative. I forget for a second that it's also kind of a pain in the butt sometimes.

"Go grab one from the hardware store next door," I tell him. "I'll pay up front."

"Hey," he says, his tone approving. He rises and shrugs his jacket over his shoulders. "Chivalry is not dead." He winks and heads toward the door to do just as I suggest, and I especially love the fact that we can be done with our Serious Talk and be normal again and there isn't so much as a speed bump hindering the shift. That's another best thing about Duncan.

It's good to have friends. Even when they are Boy Friends who aren't *Boyfriends*. It's good to have Dunc.

Now that I think about it, there are a lot of best things about Duncan. Which may be best of all.

.ıll

I'm fishing in my wallet for exact change for the bill when another good thing envelops me: the scent of musk, along with a blast of brisk air as the door to the diner opens and shuts.

"You're here," Tobin says, like he's glad about this fact, like this is amazingly fantastic news. It throws me.

"Duncan and I were hungry," I say, apologetic, though I'm not sure what I'm apologizing for. The fact that my dad just grilled him for an hour under the guise of professional research? The fact that my mom threw her crazy-ass self at him? The fact that I spend at least seventeen minutes on any given day wondering what his rough, chapped hands would feel like wrapped around my own?

The fact that, if it were possible to make Riley disappear, full-on, to evaporate into thin air, I might do it?

"Yeah," he agrees. He shifts his weight, coughs, and I wonder about his posture, why he looks the way I often feel around him. I always assumed that other people's experiences of living inside their own skin felt natural all the time. I thought I was the weirdo who couldn't ever get totally comfortable.

But maybe I thought wrong?

He says, "Your mom . . . ," and then he trails off, which is, of course, the exact perfect reason why he would be uncomfortable. *Mamacita* can have that effect on people. I should have known.

"Yeah, sorry," I say, this time completely certain of what it is I'm sorry about. "She can be a bit . . . much. And she's really embracing the whole winter-wonderland thing Denville's got going on." I shake my head. "I mean, you saw how she freaked out when you told her you were on the ski team. So you can guess what she was like when she found out about the ski section in gym class. Major spazz-o-rama. She went *insane.* Bought out the sporting goods store. It was like she willfully denied the fact that I am the least athletic person in the history of the world." Personal power walking notwithstanding, of course, but why quibble? "I haven't had the heart to tell her that I'm a hopeless case."

They say that cross-country skiing is just like walking. But I have not found any evidence to support this notion in my own practical application. Alas.

Tobin laughs. The corners of his eyes crinkle, making them sparkle. "You're not hopeless."

"Um. I can't even stay upright when we're on the floor of the *basketball court,*" I remind him. "That's sad." Because: come *on.*

"We've all been there," he insists. "It's just dumb luck that my parents strapped me into a pair of skis before I learned to talk."

The fact that he would consider this piece of information "luck" is just one of the many differences between us that highlight the whole opposites-attract theory of true love. Or so I choose to believe.

"You just need some extra lessons. Some personal attention."

Ugh. *Extra* skiing. I can think of nothing I would enjoy less.

"I could help you. I mean, I said I would. Remember? Back at the diner that day? Your mom suggested it!"

Ooh. Extra skiing with *Tobin*! That is the Best. Idea. *Ever.* I can think of nothing I would enjoy more.

Okay, score one for Mom.

Of course I remember his offering to help. I just didn't think *he'd* remember.

"Uh, yeah." My voice is just a squeak. From the corner of my eye, I see Duncan nearing the diner again, brand-new snow brush in hand. He sees me through the window of the diner, takes note of Tobin, assesses the situation, and then proceeds directly to his car without stopping in to get me.

That's my boy. Remember what I said about Duncan and Best Things?

"Yeah," I say, more forcefully this time. "Whenever."

Because, really: *whenever*. I mean, right?

Right.

"I have to help my dad out tomorrow morning," he says, "but I'm free after that."

"Ah." I can seriously barely form words. Is this conversation actually happening? Or is the falling snow somehow interfering with my brain waves? I really can't say.

Tobin mistakes my vague mutterings for ambivalence. "Or I could call you, and we could figure something out."

Call me. Awesomeness. Awesomeosity of the utmost degree.

Oh! Except—he can't call me. I don't have a phone. Whoops.

"Tomorrow's fine," I say hastily.

We make arrangements to head over to a local cross country trail, and it's too far to walk with all of our equipment, and I don't have a car, or even a license until my birthday in the spring, so it's agreed that he'll pick me up from my house after he gets off work, which is so much like a date that it doesn't even bother me when, right at the end of our planning, there's a honk from outside that Tobin tells me is Riley, waiting on him, because they're supposed to see a movie in a few minutes, and that the whole reason he was even at the diner to begin with was to pick up a couple of hot chocolates to take with them.

Obviously taking a girl to a movie *avec* hot chocolate is *also* fairly date-y, which maybe isn't the greatest news in light of my own recent Tobin-related developments-slash-fantasies. But I can't think about that now. I can't ruin the moment for myself. I just *can't.*

Because right now, at this very instant, watching snowflakes form latticework against the gray afternoon sky, certain things suddenly seem possible.

And I feel very alive.

The thing about cross-country

skiing is, it is really not at all "like walking," which is what Coach Franklin would have you believe.

Or, if it *is,* then the bad news is that, apparently, I'm not all that good at walking.

(Funny thing, that—given how much practice I've been getting, lately . . .)

I don't care. Spending the afternoon with Tobin —even strapped to a set of skis upon which I can barely balance—is worth it. *Well* worth it. This is a scientific fact.

On Sunday morning, I wake at the first crack of sunlight, which means I've "slept in" until nine-ish. Chloe would tell me just to shoot her, but I say, it could be worse, especially considering that today is my Nordic outing with the Tobinator! We had planned for him to pick me up at eleven, giving us a few hours of daylight for outdoor fun and adventure. By 10:03 I am dressed and ready to go, perched at the end of my bed and quivering with energy.

At 10:17 it occurs to me to try to eat something—wouldn't want to faint dead away from hunger in front of the dude of my dreams, however unlikely that scenario—so I make my way into the kitchen. I can't lie; I've been putting off the whole leaving-the-cocoon-of-my-bedroom thing. I'm dreading running into my mother, having to rehash the horror of the radio show. After I returned from the diner with Duncan, I managed to keep a low profile last night, begging off dinner under the guise of a stomachache, which, given the situation with the mushy cheese fries, wasn't too much of a stretch.

"You going out?" Dad peeks up at me from behind the Science section.

I nod. "Practicing skiing." I'm *thrilled* that Mom is nowhere to be found, knowing as I do how over the top her reaction to this news would be. I'm excited to be skiing—it seems like a very *cell phone* thing to do, in point of fact—but I'd never give her the satisfaction of knowing just how excited I am.

So there.

It is kind of weird that Mom's not around, though.

But, what*ever*.

So. I'm tucking into a bowl of Special K, which I normally avoid because of how the commercials are all about how totally and completely *hilarious* it is that women always think they're fat, but which in truth I actually kind of like the taste of, so it's always a whole big moral dilemma, which is really not something a person should be faced with when sitting down to the breakfast table. (I mean, it's just cereal, people.) Which is when Dad decides he's through with his reading for the time being.

"You're up early," he observes. Which, I guess I am, for a Sunday.

"Well, the skiing." Thank gawd Dad isn't the type to ask questions, or probe, or generally care about the minute details of my personal life and stuff. Seriously.

"I'm glad to see that you're establishing yourself within a peer group," he offers, pushing back from the table and heading to our fancy espresso machine to fix himself a hit. Dude is addicted to java. Though, I suppose there are worse things in life than a propensity to mainline caffeine. Things like, *establishing oneself within a peer group,* which sounds nasty and insidious, almost infectious. As though the fact that I'm making friends is almost like a disease. Like my dad is telling me, essentially, that I have cooties.

So, in summation: I've been tacitly insulted by both my high-protein cereal and my highfalutin father, and it's not even noon. As Chloe would say: just shoot me.

"Mmm-hmm . . . ," I mumble, noncommittal, through a mouthful of Special K.

(Side note: it becomes much less special the soggier that it gets.)

"Seems like your mother is adjusting to life here, too," he goes on, either unaware or unconcerned that I've not really offered much by way of a response. That my conversational skills thus far this morning have rivaled that of an inanimate object, like a step stool. Or a soupspoon. That despite my excitement at the prospect of seeing Tobin, my demeanor is only a fraction less waterlogged than my cereal.

"Huh." I'm trying not to encourage conversation, since I can barely concentrate on shoveling spoonfuls of cereal into my mouth, so focused am I on my afternoon outing, but Dad will not be denied.

"She went out to that dogsled tour place this morning, bright and early," he continues, sounding fairly bright himself. "Wanted to get some pictures in." He grabs at a dishrag and wipes down the countertop in front of the espresso machine just a tad too vigorously. "It's nice that she's really embracing this hobby. I think it's helping to fulfill her as a person while she navigates this adjustment in lifestyle."

A chunk of chewed-up cereal shoots down the wrong pipe and I erupt in a fit of coughing.

She did it. Good old Mom just went ahead and went for it: she went to Tobin's father's dogsled place. *To take pictures*. Which sounds like a euphemism for . . . I don't even want to think about what. But *something*, right?

I don't know why I'm surprised. She told us she was going to do it. And when Mom puts her mind to something, that's pretty much it. That something in question is a done deal.

I wouldn't even begrudge her this epiphany she seems to be having—this *fulfillment*, as Dad insists on terming it, anyway—if it weren't for the issue of how it overlaps ever so subtly with my own non–love life. That's where things take a sharp left turn toward Awkwardville.

But then again, the proof is in the pudding, no? (Of course, it all comes back to food. How could you doubt me?) Who knows—maybe Awkwardville can be averted. Maybe we can settle on slightly weird with a chance for a collective happy ending. I mean, she may be hoping for a behind-the-scenes look at the dogsled trade, but I'm the one heading off with Tobin for the day.

The chime of the doorbell sounds. Thank the God of Decent Timing, *Finally* (that's actually her full, official title) for small mercies.

Tobin is here. And I'm ready to go.

Ready as I'll ever be, that is.

.ıll

Like Duncan, Tobin drives an SUV, but his is a four-door that seems better suited for a true Denville winter. It's sturdier, more rugged. It's more *Tobin*, the way that Duncan's car is more Duncan, kinda like how pet owners eventually start to look like their pets, or whatever. (I'm still waiting for that to happen with Mom and Ricky Ricardo, but so far the matching outfits is as far as it goes. Small mercies, remember?)

Also like Duncan's, Tobin's car doesn't appear to be new, which is about as far as my knowledge of cars extends. It's not that my Miami friends were, like, spoiled or anything, but the truth is, I'm so used to my friends back home being given brand-spanking-new cars as sweet sixteen presents that it almost surprises me the way that secondhand is the total norm here. But I think that's another one of those epiphanies that Dad would call a "reaffirmation of perspective."

"Reaffirmations" and "perspective" are both very key to Dad. To me, not so much.

"Sorry it's such a mess," Tobin says, brushing several outdoor sports magazines and a handful of loose change off of the shotgun seat and onto the floor. We've already loaded our skis up into the back of the truck and stretched them out across the collapsed backseats, and now I hop up and scoot over into my bucket as gracefully as I can, which is to say: not very gracefully at all. I'm not sure grace and elegance are at all synonymous with snow pants, a parka, and boots that look more appropriate for a moon landing. But I'm told this is what one wears to ski. Mom would have it no other way, natch.

I go, "Oh, no . . . ," which isn't really a reply at all, and am subsequently embarrassed enough that I clasp my hands in my lap and don't say anything at all. I notice a leftover to-go mug in the cup holder that I'll bet anything is Riley's hot chocolate from yesterday, from when she and Tobin went to the movies. Which is enough of a reminder that my own outing with Tobin couldn't be further from a date to make me go utterly silent all over again.

"It'll warm up in a second," Tobin says, though I hadn't noticed a chill. It would be hard to, under the seventeen layers of down and Thinsulate that coat my body, obviously. And also, because of how just the mere fact of being within ten feet of him sends my body temperature skyrocketing.

I wonder if that's what Dad meant by *establishing myself within my peer group*—heating up involuntarily and whatnot.

My best guess? Probably not.

Tobin turns the key in the ignition. Soft indie rock fills the space between us, what Chloe would call shoegaze-y music and mean as a not-compliment. Funny, I would have pegged Tobin as a classic-rock kind of guy. Or maybe even retro grunge, what with all of the flannel, which I keep forgetting is an issue of practicality, not fashionality, up here.

He grins toward my peripheral vision, which ups my warm fuzzies by a few more degrees.

"Satellite radio," he says, as though it's a secret we share, which makes me feel lame and even guilty that it *so* isn't. "You must listen to a lot of it."

He means because of Dad's show, and—I don't know, is it weird that I *don't* listen to a lot of it? Because I don't.

I say, "Um," which also isn't really a response, but if he's thrown by my persistent inability to carry on a conversation, he's too polite to point it out, which, again: warm fuzzies.

And anyway there's soft indie rock filling up the space between us, like I say. So that's kind of a distraction. And it kind of feels, in the moment, like *everything* in between us is just as it should be.

.ıll

Tobin tells me that we're heading out to a "Nordic trail" that starts in downtown Anchorage. I'm more than slightly embarrassed to admit that this is the first time I've been to Anchorage since our plane landed a month ago, and that, also, I wasn't aware that "Nordic" skiing was, in fact, another term for cross-country skiing.

"You're kidding," Tobin says, when I tell him as much, and a blush creeps up my neck. He doesn't say it in the slangy way; he says it like he really, truly thinks I'm kidding. Which: I'm *so* not. Sadly.

I go, "Nope," and the word comes out all sharp in my mouth, and I feel like maybe I'm being flippant, even though that's not how I mean to sound. So I clear my throat, start again.

"No, I mean, I guess we've just been really busy, um, settling in, and stuff."

Busy. With the . . . settling in. And stuff.

(Side note: what stuff? Seriously, *what?* My biggest expenditure of energy since October has been living vicariously through my cell phone.)

"Yeah, well." Now Tobin's the one who sounds awkward, like he feels weird or somehow bad for putting me on the spot, even though his question was totally normal and *un*weird, really. "I guess it's a big adjustment."

Yeah. Well.

I want to tell him that the landscape of Alaska is about as foreign to me as the surface of Mars—that in Miami, when you look out the window, you see blue water, in liquid form, and blue skies, as opposed to the gray-streaked cloud formations hovering above snowcapped mountain peaks here. Miami is bright neon colors and flashing lights, and Alaska is green and robust and rugged. I want to tell him about Chloe, and how she drives a convertible, and that her hair is almost the exact same shade as Riley's, but longer, with layers that require a trip to the salon every three weeks for maintenance; to tell him that this pilgrimage is something lots of girls from my old high school do, but that Chloe does it best. And I do it only with Chloe. I want to tell him that in Miami, my family lives in a penthouse apartment with a view of the bay, which looks nothing like this place, but if you squint your eyes enough, it's not an impossibly different image from what we see, now, outside our picture window in Denville. It's not insurmountable, the gap, or inconceivable. That water is water—even when it is in an altered chemical state—and that translucence transcends.

I want to tell him that the main, true reason I haven't replaced my cell phone yet is because I'm dying, literally *dying*, in the way that curiosity supposedly killed the cat, to see what it's going to do, where it's going to go, next, and that a part of me wishes I were more like Chloe, more like Duncan, more like Riley—more like the kind of person who would *do*, rather than *watch*. More like the cat that was just so effing curious that she couldn't even help herself, consequences be damned.

I want to tell him that going with him, to Anchorage, to ski, feels a lot like *doing*. It feels scary. And exhilarating.

I want to tell him how much I want to tell him. If he were Duncan, or even Chloe, I might try. I might be able to wrap words around this feeling of breathlessness that comes from sharing Tobin's physical space. But since he *is* Tobin, I can't. I can only fiddle with the dial on the radio and nod my head, slightly out of synch with the female crooner whose voice somehow sounds exactly the way it feels inside my brain right now.

Tobin reaches over, and I lean back instinctively. I think he's going to adjust the tuner, the same way I did, just now, but at the last second, he fakes right, leans a tentative hand on my knee. And then he leans back, too.

And now the inside of my head is noisier, more crowded with bottle rockets and confetti and New Year's Eve things. The sound track inside my head is the furthest thing from indie crooning. It is fizzy, iridescent disco pop all glammed up for a sold-out stadium show. This feeling . . . it's like plunging from the tippy top of the high dive—something else, I want to tell him, I've never done.

His hand sits for a moment, then jiggles, like he's as unsure as I am, and now I want to tell him that it's okay, that I get it, that a jiggling hand is so, so, *so* much better than no hand. That a jiggling hand is, as I say, New Year's

Eve and lip gloss and red velvet cupcakes frosted with thick, sugary buttercream.

But. He clears his throat, lifts his hand off of my knee into a fist, and coughs into it.

(Between you and me: the moment that Tobin removes his hand from my knee may very well be the absolute worst, most unbearable moment of my so-called life thus far.)

I deflate, hastily begin to contemplate my makeshift exit strategies: I can leap from the car and hitchhike, snowshoe, crawl on my knees back to my house, yes? Viable Plans, all of those.

I'm considering rolling down the window and making a leap for it when Tobin turns to glance at me quickly. Something about the glint in his eyes tells me that, somehow, he can tell what I'm thinking. All of it, I mean: the New Year's Eve-y stuff, and the cupcakes, and the crawling through the snow back to my house in defeat and whatever. He heard all of the things I wanted to say. And his face—the curve of his upper lip, the edge of gold that lines his pupil, the road map of his expression—makes me feel totally naked and vulnerable and silly. But in a good way, like when you drink regular Coke from a can too quickly, and the bubbles shoot up into your nose.

That's what Tobin is: Coke bubbles shooting up into your nose. That's it. That's totally it. In a good way.

(Regular Coke, of course. The kind with the corn syrup. *Not* diet. *Major* difference, right?) I turn back at him. And I smile.

Disco bubbles, lip gloss, pop music, sugared soda.

He points past the windshield, beyond the horizon.

He says, "We're here."

..ıl

I expect Anchorage to look like a slightly larger-scale version of Denville, very small town-y, the kind of place where "shops" are suddenly "shoppes," and old men are perched on rocking chairs, smoking pipes outside of each storefront.

However, what I've neglected to factor into my fantasy is the fact that Anchorage is in *Alaska,* and that it's, you know, *November,* and I have not, in fact, stumbled onto the set of a quirky televised dramedy filming just south of the North Pole.

So basically, as we approach, Anchorage's skyline right this second looks to me essentially like that of any other biggish city, save for the fat, puffy flakes of snow floating down to the ground, which you *definitely* don't get a whole lot of in, say, Miami. Just for example.

"It's sticking," I say, meaning the snow, obviously, which Tobin clearly gets.

Although I can see how, for the average individual, the fact of the snow sticking could be seen as a positive, i.e., it would make for better skiing, both in the sense of being more picturesque and also more, you know, *fun,* to me the snow adds an extra layer of terror into our afternoon plans. If I thought it was hard "skiing" on the Traynor basketball court, well . . .

Something tells me it's all downhill from here. Even if it's not *actually* downhill skiing.

"You're going to love the Coastal Trail," Tobin says, turning smoothly. "It begins just back off of Second Avenue. Like, right in town." He says this with eyes shining and bright, like the idea of a ski trail that begins *right in town* is almost as exciting as, for instance, Chubby Hubby ice cream, which—honestly? Seems unlikely.

But shining-eyed Tobin is almost too adorable to bear, and I have to admit, there's something almost magical about the dusting of white that covers the sidewalks as we pass.

There's a moment, as he turns off of the main road again, and we head a few more yards down a wide road, and the mouth of the trail yawns before us, that I actually feel calm and secure. Eager, even. Ready to take a stab at this whole skiing thing.

Ready for almost anything.

I step out of the car and crane my face upward, shivering

as the snowflakes touch down on my face, but not feeling cold, exactly. Though I *definitely* do have the chills, it's not like I'm *chilly*; it's more like . . . I'm *anticipating*.

Tobin comes up behind me, both sets of our skis tucked under his arm. I love that he has such sturdy, broad shoulders that he can fit both sets of our skis under one arm. I mean, talk about your nice arms, right? Arms like those might even be able to wrap themselves ever so casually around my person.

I'm just sayin'.

"Shall we?" he asks, and with his free arm, he crooks my elbow through his own, like he's leading me onto a dance floor. *Swoon.*

"I'm ready," I reply. A snowflake lands squarely on the tip of my nose and I twitch to make it run off slowly.

I'm ready.

And the funniest part is?

I mean it.

Did you know that there's, like, an entire section of cross-country-ski technique dedicated to learning how to fall down properly? There totally is! And here I am, just thinking I'm a natural at that one, sad little thing, if nothing else, when it turns out there's a whole fancy way to do it, to wipe out monumentally, and really, all along, I've been just as clueless as ever.

Go figure.

"Are you feeling, you know, one with your skis?" Tobin asks. He can't quite meet my gaze as he says this, confirming that he feels like a grade-A dork asking such a question, valid though it may be. I like that about him—I like that he's in touch with his grade-A inner dork.

Oh, who are we kidding? I like *everything* about him. Come on now, people. Except for the part of him that's digging Riley, I mean.

"I . . . guess so?" I say. I try to determine what exactly "oneness with my skis" would feel like. Probably more organic, and less like I had two long wooden appendages jutting out from me perpendicularly, right? That'd be my best guess.

"The thing about cross-country is that your boots are only bound to the skis at your toes," Tobin goes on, "so you've got more flexibility." He dips at one knee, pushing one heel up in demonstration. Dude makes it look so easy! "And the skis themselves are waxed, which should make for some smooth gliding in this fresh powder."

Powder. That's lingo for the light dusting of snow that's drifting down as we prepare to take off on our alpine adventure.

I'm nothing if not a quick study.

"And then—okay, this sounds like a cliché—but the thing you want to do is, go with the flow," Tobin says. "Practice moving forward fluidly, swinging your arms and legs almost like you're walking."

I'm inspired by Tobin's voice, and his lack of inhibition re: use of cliché. I go for it (the *flow*, I mean), thrusting my torso forward and swishing one arm in front of me and one arm behind.

In my mind's eye, I envision myself slicing gracefully through the soft snowfall. Crystal flakes dance in my curls despite the fact that, in the here and now, I'm wearing a big old woolen hat that covers 80 percent of my head, not to mention my hair.

My mind's eye is very creative. And also, not a little bit delusional.

My mind's eye, frankly, is just flat-out wrong. In actuality, things go down a little bit differently.

In actuality, *I* go down. Hard.

My right hip slams into the ground, and my legs fold in the opposite direction, almost casual-like, as though I could straighten, dust off my right shoulder, cock my legs jauntily, and just be all, like, "I meant to do that."

Unfortunately, I'm way too busy trying to catch my breath—there's a shock running the length of my spine, and let me tell you, even with all of the padding that I'm wearing, landing butt-first in a pile of fresh *powder* is *cold*—for any of that.

"That was good!" Tobin enthuses.

I frown, gaze at him skeptically. *Yeah,* I want to say, *that was some good doing it wrong. High marks! I am awesome at screwing things up!*

And also: kind of a klutz. For real.

"No, I'm serious. Falling properly is a whole technique. You're supposed to stay low to the ground, tilt your hips to one side, and land on your—" He cuts off abruptly, looking embarrassed.

"Big fat butt?" I finish for him brightly.

He says nothing, but hovers over me, reaching a hand out

and helping me to my feet. I drop my poles to the ground on either side of my body and set about brushing off my aforementioned big fat butt.

Now that we're essentially face-to-face, it's clearer to me that Tobin's cheeks are fire-engine red.

"You're not . . . I mean, your butt isn't . . ." His face flares neon at the word *butt*, and he looks like he wants to dig a hole in a snowdrift and crawl into it to die.

I can relate. I've been there. But, hey—if we can't be realistic about my butt, then what have we got left in this world, anyway?

"It's fine," I assure him. "This is one of those times when the extra padding is a blessing, you know?" I even pat at my own backside for good measure. It's so fine that it doesn't even occur to me when being self-effacing became a casual thing and not an utter revelation of my inner (well, outer, really) angst and my nonspecific self-loathing.

Tobin laughs slightly louder and longer than a normal person would, betraying his nerves. The thought that I can make Tobin nervous feels deliciously empowering. No wonder the size of my butt has shifted to one of the absolute least of my concerns, ever.

(Side note: OMG, *really*?!)

"You're a good teacher," I say, mainly because it's something to say. Even if I never, ever improved at skiing even one single iota, he'd still be my favoritest, most bestest teacher ever.

He shrugs. "So far all I've done is watch you fall."

Who can be bothered with such trivialities as the cold, hard facts? I shake my head no. "But, you were really supportive about that, so, you know—gold star."

He laughs, more naturally this time, showing all his teeth, and the sight of his expression feels like slipping my bare toes into warm sand on a day that is the opposite of today, weather-wise.

I had not known that it was possible to feel that way, all beachy-keen and whatever, amid snow flurries. But now that I think about it, it makes perfect sense. Flurried: that's how I feel.

"I've been doing it for a long time," he says, almost like an apology, like he feels guilty for being less of a spazz than I am.

Adorable.

"Actually—there's going to be a competition in two weeks," he says. "Ski team, you know? The weekend of Thanksgiving: that Saturday."

"I might have heard something about that," I say, even though: no.

I've been trying to avoid the whole subject of Thanksgiving entirely. Mom wants to go back to Miami, spend it with her extended Cuban family (and in her defense, *Tío* Ramon's fried plantains are the bomb), but the studio offered Dad *mucho dinero* to do a special on coping with sudden-onset holiday depressyitis.

(That's obviously not, like, the clinical term for it.)

"Well, you should come." Right. Tobin's ski-competition thingy.

Oh, hey now. *Waitaminute*. Is Tobin, like, *inviting* me to his ski-competition thingy? Or is he just, you know, inviting me to his ski-competition thingy?

It makes a difference, you know—the implied italics.

In this case, the intonation is everything. I can't tell you how much I hope it's the former, hope that it's implied italics with little hearts over the *i*'s and written in silver glitter pen. Or I guess I can—I *have*—told you.

I guess it was never really a secret, anyway.

"Everyone's going to be there," Tobin says. "It's, like, a thing around here."

Oh. Right. *Everyone*. So: no italics for Aggie.

He goes on, twisting the knife further. "Riley and her friends are competing, too."

"Awesome," I say weakly. Riley may be the absolute bestest, most perfect gal in the universe, but:

1) She is sort of my arch nemesis, in that she's got that "connection" with Tobin that I just can't hear enough about,

and

2) I can't pretend that some of her friends aren't horrible. (Well, okay, just the one friend, really. But she's *awful*. Just thinking about Tegan makes me shudder.)

Talk about your sudden-onset depressyitis. It feels like a sucker punch to my solar plexus, like if I were even sure of where exactly my solar plexus is, because: *everyone's going to be there.* Meaning, there's nothing special at all, *whatsoever,* about his having mentioned it to me. One might even consider it an act of charity.

Pfft.

I square my shoulders, try to loosen up. Forget it, anyway. All of the best, most epic-est crushes of all time have been unrequited. That's a scientific fact. I'll take any Tobin I can get, even if I'm stalling out in the Friend Zone.

"Show me that wedge turn thing that Coach Franklin was going on about," I say, grabbing at my poles again and somehow managing to push off and move toward him without wiping out again. Miraculous!

"All right," he says. "We'll do the wedge turn, and then some hills."

I am about to protest—hills sound difficult, and I am decidedly anti anything difficult—when he finishes, "And then maybe the diner? For some hot chocolate? If you want."

If I want. "All right."

More than all right.

I think: *I may still be shamefully undersmooched, as far as teenage girls go, but there is hot chocolate on the horizon.*

There are worse things in the world.

..ıl

We abandon the ski lesson once it gets dark, which: three-fifteen-ish. By then, I'm ready for hot chocolate and also something more substantive, like a cheeseburger deluxe. (The platter, not the plate.) My stomach grumbles as our car rumbles along. As long as I'm stuck in the Friend Zone with the T-man, why the heck not devour twice my body weight?

I mean, seriously.

But as Tobin is parking the car, there's a chirping sound from his pocket. He reaches in and fishes out a cell phone. It's more basic than mine, but it does the trick—the screen on the flip top says RILEY CALLING.

Oh, joy.

Tobin snaps the phone open and holds it up to his ear. "Hey. Yeah. Just finished the lesson now. We're at the diner, gonna get something to eat . . ." He pauses, and underneath his breathing I can hear the tinny echo of Riley's side of the conversation, though I can't make out her words exactly. He glances at me sideways. "Yeah, you should come. Join us."

No, you shouldn't. I am a terrible person.

"It's totally fine."

No, it isn't. I am evil and small.

"We're just going to have a quick bite, and then I'm going to take Aggie home. You've got me all to yourself tonight."

At that, I am consumed with *meh*. Beside Tobin in the passenger seat, I squeeze my eyes shut, dizzy. He is going to be with Riley tonight. She's going to have him *all to herself*. He and I are *just having a quick bite*.

Like I say: *meh*. Raised to the power of *woe is me*.

I mean, there's the Friend Zone, and then there's flat-out setting yourself up for a heart-in-meat-grinder experience. I don't really need to spend thirty minutes stuffing my face with Tobin, knowing the whole time that he's just counting the seconds down until he can get to his *real* date.

I tug at Tobin's arm. "Uh, you know, it's fine," I say. "I'm . . . not that hungry after all."

Tobin peers at me. "Hang on," he says to Riley, cupping his palm over the phone's mouthpiece. To me, he goes, "Are you sure?"

"Yeah." *No.* Although the fact that he isn't trying all that hard to keep me here goes a long way toward that certainty I'm craving. "I can just walk home. I need some fresh air, anyway."

Good one, Aggie. Smooth. 'Cause the three hours of fresh air you just had while skiing with Tobin *were* obviously *not sufficient. Whatever.*

Meh, woe, and—ooh, here's a new one: *blergh*.

"What about your skis?" Tobin asks, clearly torn.

I have to make this easy for him. I mean, one of us should have it easy in this equation, right? "I can get them from you after school tomorrow. Don't worry about it."

Before he can protest further, I unlock my door and slide out. "Thanks!" I say, forcing myself to sound vaguely chipper. "It was fun! Next week, definitely!"

Tobin looks dazed, which is kind of how I feel. He takes a breath, then says, "Right."

And I don't even have time to hope that he means it before he turns back to his phone call, turns back to Riley.

CHAPTER 16

Picture it:

still life with lovelorn teen.

Mom has come back from her own winter outing revived and filled with purpose. Apparently, the dogsled tour was three tons of fun. Tobin's father showed her the ropes.

The irony of our situation is, of course, not lost on me: my mother had a better "date" with Tobin's father than I did with Tobin himself.

Meh, woe, blergh, indeed.

If Mom is clued in to my funk at all, she chooses to ignore it, instead weaving circles around my perch on our leopard-print club chair, fiddling with the zoom lens on her camera.

"Mom," I snap, "come *on*. I'm not in the mood. I'm tired."

"Fine, fine," she trills, choosing to breeze past the brat-tastic tone in my voice, "you can just sit there like the bump on the log." She presses down with her finger and captures me in all of my sullen misery. I glare, but she isn't deterred.

"These *fotografías*, I tell you—they will be *absolutmente perfecto* for the gallery show."

"*Fantastico*."

Except, wait. What?

I rise from the chair, place my hands at my hips. "Wait. *What?*"

She giggles like a schoolgirl. The sound could shatter crystal.

"Didn't I tell you? One of the ladies from the *e-spin* class, she works at the *biblioteca*. She likes to hang work by local artists in the foyer. It's her gallery, she calls it. And she's going to showcase *mi* photos," Mom says proudly, like someone has offered to hang her little snapshots in the Guggenheim, instead of just in the front entryway to the Denville Free Public Library.

"It will be fun," she says, grinning madly and totally ignoring the expression on my face that suggests that *fun* is the absolute last thing this latest manufactured drama will be. "It will be like a big *fiesta*, fancy gallery opening, you know? Your father has already said that he will talk it up on his radio show." Now she is the one who looks me over, takes me in. "We'll get you something new to wear for the party."

"Whatever." Maybe I'd be able to muster some enthusiasm for this new development if it weren't happening in tandem with the final death rattle of my Tobin crush. Or barring that possibility, if, say, my mother were able to scrounge herself up a nice sensible pair of Mom jeans, or the like.

Maybe. It's hard to say.

Has the entire world gone completely crazy-pants? Or is it just me?

Seriously. Inquiring minds want to know. Maybe there's medication for this state of being, or something.

"I think . . . something in a bright *naranja*," Mom goes on, chirping away as though all is as perky and perfect as ever. Still focused on the problem of what I will be wearing to her *fiesta*. "*Perfecto* for you." Even though nothing ever was anything remotely approaching perky or perfect to begin with.

Okay, now I have to say something. *Naranja* = *no dice*. I roll back toward Mom's trilling voice again.

"You know I don't wear citrus—"

I stop, midsentence.

She's already gone.

.ıll

So, I've been thinking.

Wondering, really. It would be more accurate to say that I've been wondering.

What would my cell phone do?

I've been abandoned, forsaken, left to stew, to wither within my own questionable choices. Completely cast aside by the various deities I've known and semirespected at one point or another: the God of Ill-Conceived Timing, the God of Bad Outfits, the God of Unrequited Lurve and Crushage . . .

What have they done for me lately?

Nada. Zip. Zilch.

Well. I've never been much for organized religion, anyway.

Which brings us back to my original question, the one that I'm hoping will open up a whole new door to consciousness. Since this voluntary unconsciousness thing I've been cultivating for the last few years has certainly not been doing me any favors.

My cell phone, it seems, has it all figured out. We've talked about this, you and I. My cell phone is going places.

And I'm going to go there, too.

From here on in, my cell phone is Goddess. And I'm her loyal supplicant. She's got the right idea. And now I do, too.

Once I free myself from Mom's roving camera lens, something inside my brain just clicks. There are so few things in this world over which I have any control. I couldn't even keep ahold of my oh-so-aspiring cell phone, for jeezum's sake. But. I'm gonna work that out. Tweak it to my advantage. Things are going to change around here for good old Aggie Eckhart. As my cell phone goes, so goes my nation.

You'll see.

.ıll

First things first: track that sucker down. Easy enough. A few taps on my keyboard, and I'll know what exactly that little imp has been up to. So far, she's hit Bob's Wilderness Tours, the bird-watching place, and Young-Brenner Dogsled. I can only imagine what's on the agenda for this afternoon.

The little hourglass does its spinny thing on the computer screen while I drum my fingers against my desktop. I imagine this is what gamblers feel like as the roulette wheel turns. Except, I swear, the stakes are higher for me here, now.

Whammo.

I lean forward in my seat, eager to see where fate will soon be taking me. Snowshoeing through the Alaskan Alps (are there even Alaskan Alps?)? Glacier hopping? Skinny-dipping à la the Polar Bear Club?

Come on . . . come on . . .

Come . . .

On . . . ?

I blink, shake my head, do a double take.

My cell phone, it seems, is at Katie's Krew Kuts, off of Route 23. I quickly check out their Web site. Apparently, they're running a special on wash and blowouts for three days only.

(Side note: whoever's got my cell phone sure is hitting the town with it. Though, I guess I have only myself to blame, what with how I haven't bothered to report it missing, or cancel the account, or do anything even remotely proactive with it. And stuff.)

And so, yeah, I haven't had so much as a bang trim since we left Florida, about six weeks ago, now, and maybe I am starting to cultivate the whole homeless-vagrant look, but still. Still. A haircut isn't exactly the adventure that I was expecting when I decided to adopt the whole cell-phone scavenger hunt.

Okay, then. No problemo. On to Plan B.

What was the second-to-last place that my cell phone visited?

Survey says: the Eagle River Nature Center.

Forty-five minutes from downtown Anchorage, a variety of hikes led by trained experts. Scenery is described (by the Interwebs, that is) as "breathtaking," and the center is the gateway to the Chugach State Park.

(Side note: it is accessible by public transportation, too. Bonus!)

"Breathtaking." That sounds about right.

Okay, I'm in.

.ıl

There's this little pounding that happens, not quite in your head but not quite in your throat—more like somewhere just in between, in that soft space behind your ears. It's the pulse of blood rushing, of exertion and energy and push. It happens only when you're straining, moving. Working. That much, I know. Now.

About a month ago, when I first started walking to and from town in the mornings, that pounding was unfamiliar and new. Unsettling. It drained me.

Now, though?

Now it fills me up.

The guide grins at me crookedly, exhales. "I'm going to have to work to keep up with you, I can tell," he tells me, not unpleasantly.

And you know something, folks?

He's right.

CHAPTER 17

"So let me get this straight,"

Duncan says, doodling a little crosshatch on the cover of his notebook from his seat next to me in Markman's class. "You're trying to convince me that there's something Zen about the way your heart beats when you get all sweaty and flushed from athletic exertion." He says "Zen" the way you might say "cooties" or "STD," making a face like he's just smelled something rancid. Actually, he kind of looks a little bit like Tegan Darcy right now.

I don't mean that as a compliment, by the way. Just in case you were wondering.

I nod. "Correct." Oh, but: "Except, it's not athletic exertion, really. It's just hiking." These days, I can tell the diff. Go, me! And, *thank you, cell phone.*

Duncan arches an eyebrow at me dubiously. "Forgive me, darling. But hiking sounds not terribly unlike exercise. You can see where I might be confused."

Fair enough. "There *may* be a physical component to

the process," I concede. "But it's worth it. I'm telling you, there's that little drumbeat thing that happens—"

"Please, for the love of your well-worn *h*'Uggs, Aggie," Duncan stage-whispers, cutting me off, "spare me the part about how your eardrums throb and you go into some kind of ecstatic state."

If Duncan was agnostic before, I've pushed him well over the threshold toward the dark vortex of nonbelief. But I can't say as I feel particularly guilty about it.

"Fine." I cross my arms, slightly miffed. From the front of the classroom, Markman shoots us a look, possibly also slightly miffed. Which is fair.

"I guess you know all there is to know about meditative experiences." My tone implies that I do not believe this to be the truth. Because, I mean: really.

"Well, you'll forgive me for not embracing your new attitude without some reservations, especially given as how you're suddenly *taking orders from your lost cell phone*," Duncan snits, his voice rising in pitch. I flatten my hand and press it down in front of him, the universal gesture for *take it down, dude,* reminding him that Markman isn't completely oblivious, unfortunately.

I say, "I'll make you a deal."

"As if you've got any bargaining power here." Duncan sniffs.

"I'll leave you alone. I'll never mention the whole pounding-heartbeat, blood-throbbing-in-the-eardrums thing again—"

"*Perf.*" Duncan cuts me off tersely with a pert smirk. "I accept your deal. You had me at 'leave you alo—'"

"*If* you come with me on one, single cell-phone-designated outing."

Check and mate.

Now it's my turn to look smug. If his perplexed expression is anything to go by, I've got Dunc right where I want him.

He wrinkles his nose. "But *where*?"

I sigh lightly, with great worldliness. "That's the magic of it all. We won't know until we consult the cell phone. It is the great scavenger hunt of chance. And GPS."

"The cell phone is all-knowing." Duncan's voice drips with scorn.

"*Now* you're getting it," I say, brightly.

I feel the thrumming cueing up again, deep within my veins, but I refrain from sharing this fact with Duncan. I can tell the boy's hanging on by a thread. But at least he's agreed to my terms. For now. For now, *I'm* in the driver's seat.

Metaphorically speaking, but still:

Progress, baby.

▪▫▬

So, we cut school.

It's out of our hands—the cell phone tells us we must. Therefore, we must. It is simply that straightforward. We have no choice.

The day cruise of Prince William Sound takes just over four hours, and it's about a two-and-a-half-hour drive from Denville. It's a good thing my boy Dunc has wheels, and a total disregard for his attendance record.

It's also a good thing neither of us is prone to seasickness.

In all seriousness, though, the *Klondike Express* cruiser is an impressive vessel. Once it gets going, the wind whips against our cheeks like rubber bands.

"Did you know the sound is protected?" Duncan asks, leaning close and cupping his hands around his mouth so that I can hear him.

I shake my head. "I knew nothing of the sound prior to this excursion," I remind him primly. "That is why we are here."

"Broad horizons are *so* important," Duncan replies, positioning himself against the guardrail in a king-of-the-world posture that earns him a look from yours truly. Which earns *me* a look that reminds me that we've got Duncan's father's credit card ("He never checks the statement—it would be an act of actual 'active parenting'") to thank for our little jailbreak.

As our boat chugs out toward the glacier range, our guide, a portly type in a vibrant life vest, chatters on about the native Alaskan culture. Duncan makes hand-puppet blah-blah-blah gestures from hip level, but I can tell that he's digging being outside for the afternoon, despite the decided nip in the air. I know he also enjoys slipping one past his father now and then. Which certainly makes enough sense.

I elbow him in the ribs. "Broad horizons are so important."

He's just about to come back with a quip—I can see it in his eyes—when the engine cuts out and our boat slows, rocking gently back and forth.

"The harbor seals bring their pups out here," our guide explains, life vest flashing like a beacon. "It's a floating nursery." A throng of tourists rush forward toward the edge of the railings, making me glad Duncan was aggressive in setting us up there from the beginning, blue lips and numb fingernails or no.

A floating nursery. It's freakin' amazing, is what it is. The baby seals on the glacier are slick, their coats mottled and their eyes wide and expressive. I'd swap Ricky Ricardo for one of these puppies in a heartbeat. (Sorry, Ricky-O, but it's the truth.) Something about their soulful gazes is like a sucker punch to the throat. Or so I'd imagine, having lived a fairly uneventful and sucker-punch-free sixteen years.

Glaciers are unbelievable, I learn. They are literally not to be believed.

Glaciers are one of the most elemental forms, distilled and sustained through time. They are strong and cold and hard as glass, and they dot the water like beads plucked from a broken strand of pearls.

I learn that glaciers form when snow and ice thicken to the point that they have no choice but to move. That the pressure has built up in such a way that the snowy surface can't help but drift. It has been that way forever and ever. Pressure builds, masses thicken, and things drift.

And as they move, they look like diamonds.

They're rooted, though. A lot of the time, they're rooted. Their stems, or whatever the real, science-y word is for them— they go down far, way beneath the surface of the water, the jewel facet of bubbling blue that you can see with your eyes.

Continental drift happens slowly, in aeons-long incre- ments. But pressure builds, masses form, and forward momentum is set into motion.

It makes sense to me.

■ııl

Watching the sun touch down over the horizon, pouring frac- tured prisms of stained-glass color across the satin-smooth surface of the glacial plane, feels almost like a cosmic do-over, like the kind of thunderstorm that leaves a brilliant rainbow in its wake. It's . . . well, it's Zen in a way that might almost be described as ecstatic, trancelike. Even though I promised Duncan I wouldn't use those words anymore.

I can tell that Duncan agrees with me, too, because he doesn't say one single word on our car ride back. We don't even listen to music, just stare straight ahead at the lines of the roadway as they roll smoothly beneath the Jeep and behind us, pushing us forward and home again.

It's dark out when Duncan pulls into my driveway. He lets the car idle, but doesn't kill the ignition. I wonder what's happening in the space behind his ears, what exactly his heartbeat is doing at this precise moment, but I don't want to ask, don't want to spoil the pristine silence. To mention it would be like skipping stones across one of those cloudy glacier surfaces just as the sunset is exploding in brilliant gold.

Duncan clears his throat, but doesn't turn to me. "Thanks," he says, barely blinking. Barely breathing. There is nary a snit to be detected in his aura.

Do I know my boy, or do I know my boy?

"Welcome." I reach for the door handle. Then I pause.

"You know," I add, almost as an afterthought, "the color of your eyes is like the surface of the water. Just underneath where the ice begins." Because it is.

All at once, I wonder:

What would my cell phone do?

For real, now. Talk to me, cellie.

I know this: it certainly wouldn't pine after a boy who was otherwise spoken for, that's for darn tootin'. And if I know my cell phone, it probably wouldn't waste any time mooning and sulking when there are plenty of other . . . uh . . . seal pups on the glacier face. Or whatever.

My cell phone would grab a cute-faced boy by the lapels of his charcoal peacoat and make its own fate happen. It would laugh in the face of the God of Platonic Relationships.

Chloe, too, would tell me to do it. I know she would. And wasn't it Duncan himself who said that the cell phone was all-knowing? I decide to test that theory.

I take a deep breath, and dive forward, aiming for Duncan's lip region like a heat-seeking missile. There's a hitch, a fraction of a nanosecond, where the air between us ripples, and then, *whammo*—full-frontal lip lockage.

Duncan makes a small squeaking sound and wrenches backward.

Duncan. *Makes a squeaking sound.* He *squeaks.*

I need to die. Like, pronto. *Immediamente.* NOW.

"Aggie," Duncan says, breathing heavily, "what was that?"

The fact that he even has to ask, that my own kissing skills are so minimal as to require further explanation, is too sad to contemplate. I need to go live on an ice floe with the seal babies. That's obviously my only remaining recourse.

But Duncan is still waiting for an answer. And the ice floe is, like, a two-hour drive away.

"A kiss," I say, finally. "That was a kiss."

Duncan rolls his eyes, which seems even more impossibly insensitive, but who even knows, at this point, what normal is, seeing as how I just spontaneously decided to maul my best friend at the imagined recommendation of an electronic device, and all. So maybe I'm not the best judge of rational, thoughtful behavior.

"Duh. *Obviously* that was a kiss. What I mean is, *why* was that a kiss?"

Unsurprisingly, I have never been asked to justify a kiss before, and I find I cannot think of a proper response. Instead, I simply shrug, wishing I could retract my head into my shoulders like a turtle, make the entire world disappear.

Duncan lays a hand on the back of my neck. "Aggie," he says, quieter now, "I thought you knew."

What now? I wonder. *Knew what?*

'Cause I swear to the God of Unintended Irony, if he tells me he's been dating Tegan this whole time, I'm going to run away and join a dogsled team myself. That is one piece of

information that I simply will not be able to process. No way, Jose.

"Aggie," Duncan says, cutting into my reverie. "I'm *gay.*"

Who in the what, now?

I turn to him, my mouth forming a perfect O, utterly dumbfounded. Memories rush together like the final scene in an M. Night Shyamalan movie. I try to seize that one crystallized moment, that unique, specific detail that would send all other clues sliding into place like matched cherries on the window of a slot machine.

I can't say it was obvious, but . . . Duncan and I were *friends.*

How could I possibly have missed something this big?

You weren't looking, Aggie, I think. *You were too focused on your feelings for Tobin, the dropping temperatures, your missing cell phone—anything but someone other than yourself.*

It's official, then: I am a terrible, horrible, person. I *am.*

"I swear, Aggie, I thought you knew. I mean, everyone knows. It's not a secret." Duncan looks mortified, and terrified that I'll be angry, that I'll feel misled.

He is the one who is worried here.

I am a crappy friend.

"Holy schnieke, Dunc," I say, shaking my head in disbelief. "I am the worst. The absolute worst."

He turns to me, laughing a little bit. I can tell he is relieved. I am, too. We both know it's going to be okay between us. Better than okay—and even better than before.

"I can't believe I just sexually harassed my best friend," I say. "I'm the worst."

"No, you're not," Duncan insists.

And hugs me.

Ricky Ricardo's beady black eyes greet me as I push through the front door, nervous and accusatory all at once. He's wearing nothing save for a slim leather collar, and the poor thing looks naked, relatively speaking.

(Side note: I may have lost touch with perspective vis-à-vis: appropriate levels of dress for members of the canine species.)

"What are you so cranky about?" I ask him lightly, not really expecting much of an answer.

Then I step into the dining room.

My mother, it seems, has littered our oversized Philippe Starck–style table with snapshots from her day with Christopher Young. It's like a deranged collage, a visual assault. Some images are black-and-white, some are vibrant Technicolor, but all wink up as though they're looking directly at me. As though they can see straight through to my very soul.

Frankly, my soul would prefer a little more privacy.

I feel the way Ricky Ricardo looks. It's like someone has shoved a fist down my throat and squeezed my insides. It's like getting your insides wrung out like a towel. It's like a Nordic-ski wipeout that starts at your butt bone and rattles straight through to your molars. (Trust me, I would know.)

In the foreground, one snapshot dangles precariously off of the corner of the table. I inch toward it slowly, suspicious, eyes narrowed.

My mother must have set a timer for this beauty.

In it, she and a man who has hair the exact shade as Tobin's (I can tell, even in black-and-white) beam out at an imaginary eye.

They're . . .

Well, the word *ecstatic* comes to mind again.

They look happy. Refreshed.

They look—*oh, ew*—as though they belong together.

I can't believe she'd leave this picture out, with the rest of them, on the dining room table, just waiting for my father or for me to come home and find it.

Or maybe that was the plan all along?

In the words of dear old *paterfamilias*: *classic passive-aggressive behavior*, no?

It's times like these I'm relieved not to have a cell phone anymore. Clearly, it's not as though I can call Tobin about this. And Chloe—well, I think I want to wait a while before giving her the full debrief on my adventure with Duncan today.

And as for Duncan himself, I'd hate to harsh his Zen, you know? Even though I know he'd be more than willing to listen. Duncan had a very transformative experience this afternoon, and I don't want to intrude on that. No matter how much I may want to bury myself in the nearest accessible igloo as soon as would be humanly possible.

That would be a very un-cell-phone thing to do, I think. Bugging Duncan, I mean. My cell phone is way more independent than that.

So that's not how I'm doing things, these days.

.ıl

I chop carrots like I want to cause them pain.

"Aggie," my father says, "what did that salad ever do to you?"

Mom's off at the library, working away on the plans for her "gallery opening," as she grows more and more psychotic— oh, excuse me, *enthusiastic*—about her photography. By which I mean: Dad and I have been spending a lot more quantity time together, doing things like preparing dinner so that it's ready when her Be-Sequinedness comes home.

I glance down at my cutting board; it's true that the carrots have been diced so finely that they're practically a puree. I don't care; I just continue to slice and dice away angrily. It's kind of therapeutic, in a twisted sort of way. Dad of all people should get that, right?

"It's just— I don't understand why it doesn't bother you. How much time she's been spending taking her dumb pictures and stuff. I mean, how exciting could it possibly be, anyway?"

"It's healthy for your mother to explore new hobbies," Dad says, using his even, measured "radio" voice.

I hate that stupid voice.

"Alaska is uncharted territory for her. She's testing the waters."

"Alaska is uncharted territory for *all* of us," I remind him. *And you don't see the rest of us dashing off on exotic new quasi-romances. Unfortunately.* "Also, you're mixing metaphors."

My father sighs, puts aside the dish towel that he's been wiping across the granite countertop for the last fifteen minutes or so.

(Side note: "preparing dinner" usually equals my cooking, FYI. Just so we're clear on that. Turns out, I'm pretty handy with a skillet and a wooden spoon.)

"I don't know what to tell you, Aggie. Your mother's

fine. I'm fine. We are fine when we're together, and it's fine that we've been spending some time apart."

I notice that he doesn't ask how *I'm* doing.

Me? Oh, I'm just fine, too, thank you.

Ha!

Kind of okay, anyway. I mean, Duncan's the best; Tobin's okay as a friend, if I have to settle on the nonideal platonic; and on Tuesday, I followed my cell phone snowshoeing down the Anchorage Flattop Mountain Trail. The view was dazzling, dizzying.

I guess that was a little bit more than fine, I have to admit to myself. Even if my father doesn't seem to care at all about how—or even what—I've been doing.

"Besides," Dad cackles fiendishly, in a very un-Dad-like manner. "The library show is the only way I could convince her to stick around for Thanksgiving."

I look up sharply. "What do you mean?" I've been dreading the library "show" for various reasons, which should all be fairly obvious, but this sounds significantly more ominous. Consider my curiosity officially piqued.

"The show. It's that Saturday, of Thanksgiving weekend. So she's agreed to skip out on *Tío* Ramon's heart attack on a plate just this once." He beams, clearly very proud of himself. Fair enough: it's a cunning plan.

But.

Saturday.

The same day as Tobin's ski-competition thingy. That I wasn't even sure he wanted me at. That I wasn't even sure I wanted to go to.

That I so totally *have* to go to.

Oh, crudness.

"Aggie!"

My father's voice startles me, shakes me out of my reverie. He tosses his dish towel into the sink and rushes to my side. "You're bleeding."

I glance down at my index finger—so I am. That's what I get for taking out my frustrations at the world on a pile of innocent vegetables.

Funny, it doesn't even hurt. Is this what shock feels like?

Dad rushes my hand to the sink, runs it under the cold water until my finger is practically numb. He examines the wound. "I don't think it needs stitches," he says, sounding relieved.

"Of course not." Though it'll be a while before my next manicure. Now I'm feeling slightly dizzy, although it might just be from the sight of the blood. Things that are meant to be inside your skin should really stay there. Inside. Ew.

Dad wraps my now-clean finger up in the dish towel tightly, squeezes. "Keep applying pressure," he says.

I do, and eventually the dizziness clears and the numbness

in my finger gives way to a dull throb that Dad says a little Tylenol with codeine should cure. I demur, thinking the unleaded will be just fine for my purposes. It's not like I'm an amputee, after all. It's just a minuscule meal-related mishap. I stick with the generic ibuprofen like the stoic, spartan Zen master I've become.

Like my cell phone, I am *so* hard-core.

Obviously, I'm off dinner duty for the rest of the evening. Dad says we can order a pizza, which I know will send Mom into a fit, which is all the more reason to be excited about it. I ask for extra cheese, and watch as Dad dumps the watery carrot slog into the trash can under the sink. I slump down at the kitchen table, keeping my arm extended in front of me, clutching away at my dish towel, watching ever-tinier flowers of red bloom every few moments or so. The bleeding has slowed.

Applying pressure. Sometimes, it works.

Sometimes, the solution is really that simple.

Sometimes.

CHAPTER 19

Naturally, Mom reacts to the pizza like it's nuclear, like it will fuse directly to her thighs if she so much as sits in the same room with it. Like you can inhale the grease through tiny molecules of air.

Naturally, this prompts me to eat two extra slices.

Say cheese, Mom, I think, chewing furiously. *Extra-extra-extra cheese.*

.ıll

It's not an hour later that I'm crippled with extra-extra-*extra* stomach cramps. Mental note: stuffing my face = *really* not the best way to plot revenge against the parentals.

I crawl under my covers with my laptop, thinking about my almost-sister. The one who was going to fulfill all of my mother's wildest expectations. The one who never was. There's that whole theory of chain reactions, of the impact of chaos, of the momentum that builds from one action to another. If I'd had that sister, what might have been different for me?

It's not that I hate my life, you know—not *all* of it, anyway—or that I wish *I'd* never been born. I just don't see, exactly, why my parents bothered if all they were going to do, all my mother was going to do, was spend her time enumerating to me all of the varied ways in which I constantly fall short of her expectations. If I'd had a sister, maybe Mom would cut me some slack now and then—if not ignore me entirely.

"*Agacita,* you should take more care of your body. Is not good not to get the *h*'exercise."

"*Agacita,* you should wear more color. Who wants to spend her life looking like a backdrop?"

"*Agacita,* you are so quiet!"

"*Agacita,* you like too much to be alone. I think if it were not for Chloe, you'd never leave the *casa!*"

What's wrong with that? I think, urgently, fervently. *What's wrong with wanting to blend in, to fade out? What's wrong with wanting to go unnoticed?*

Nothing. Another voice pipes up, this one pulled from some secret, hidden trapdoor part of my brain. *There's nothing wrong with that at all . . .*

Or, rather, there wouldn't *be.*

If you weren't 178 percent Full. Of. It. In major denial.

Like, completely and totally lying to your big fat self.

Huh. Hidden trapdoor voice cuts straight to the chase, it would seem. She's all about the tough love.

I'm not into it.

For the past sixteen years, after all, I've been pretending that volunteering to be the sidekick, the runner-up—the funny, fat best friend—was a choice. That it had to do with anything other than fear.

I've been pretending that I am the sister who lived.

Even though I've steadfastly refused to get a life.

Well, excuse me, hidden trapdoor voice, but I think you're forgetting a little mantra I've recently adopted. Namely: *What would my cell phone do?* Yeah, so at first, it was almost like a game, a dare to myself, but what I've been thinking of as a bass-ackward sort of scavenger hunt is lately, really, kind of . . . a search for my*self.*

And okay—maybe I've gotten kind of good at lying to myself, at delusion and stuff, but the real, honest-to-Godiva truth of the matter is this:

I like what I've been finding.

A lot.

Myself, she's not so bad, when you get to know her.

..ıl

The aurora borealis was named after the Roman goddess of dawn, Aurora. It is a band of light that streaks across the sky in bizarre hues of glowing greenish-red, as if aliens were invading up at the North Pole, or the sun were accidentally rising inside out. You can see it from the outer edge of town, from the lookout point that runs down the hill at the end of our street.

So I do.

It's wacky. And suddenly very easy to imagine that I'm an extra in a B-movie sci-fi flick. Which is awesome.

But still: *inside out*. That's how I feel right now. And not just because I had to set my alarm for the crack of holy jeez in order to see the northern lights in their full, twinkly glory. These days, I'm a morning person, it seems, which is weird enough, sure. But the electric-mixer-in-my-rib-cage sensation has more to do with a general sense of confusion than any inner-body-clock thing.

I don't know how to make it stop.

I don't know how to make anything happen the way that I want it to.

I don't know what, if anything, to say to my mother.

I blink, and a flash of light rockets across the skyline. A shooting star? A meteor?

The cell-phone part of me wants to believe that it's one or the other. That whatever I've just seen is magic, something a person could wish upon, if he or she were so inclined.

But.

The regular, boring, old-skool Aggie part of me, the one that tried to push aside the hidden, trapdoor voice the other night? Well, *that* girl thinks that a blurry burst in the sky is probably just an airplane or whatever. Something boring like that.

Gawd.

That part of me is such a drag.

In my mind, I give her a shove, bolt forward, leap past her, and sprint off.

(Side note: my inner cell phone is quite the athlete.)

I flip a brain coin and call it.

I decide:

I'll go to my mother's show.

My inner cell phone would be so proud. Right?

CHAPTER
20

We give Thanks.

It goes mainly like this:

I am thankful that Ricky Ricardo's Native American headdress has vanished mysteriously (I had nothing to do with it. Swearsies.) and that he must therefore spend the afternoon naked as the day he was born.

My mother, less so.

I am thankful that Mom's "gallery" preparations mean that she's suddenly all kinds of MIA, meaning that I am free to cell phone hop and generally enjoy myself without constant fear of being spontaneously captured on film.

My father is mostly thankful for carbohydrates, and the one day of the year that Mom lets him eat as many of them as he wants.

So, yeah. Thanksgiving.

Whatever.

▄▄▊▊

"Oh my god, it's just like opening night at the Factory!"

I have to say, in light of recent discoveries, Duncan's borderline obsession with Andy Warhol is making a lot more sense.

I pinch him. "You have to be nice.".

"Why?"

"Because one of us does. And it is definitely *not* going to be the me of us." I consider his comment further for a moment. "Besides, I don't think the Factory worked like a regular museum and stuff. I don't think Andy Warhol ever had an opening night."

"You don't *think*. But you don't *know*, either. You are not an expert on Warhol or the modern art movement. So. I am going to stand by my snark."

I roll my eyes.

Of course he's going to stand by his snark. He wouldn't be Duncan otherwise, and that's why I love him. Also, I have to cut him some slack, since I totally guilted/bullied him into accompanying me to Mom's "show." I know he's had his eye on one of Tobin's ski buddies lately (Kurt/Adam! Whose name, it turns out, is actually Patrick!), and I bet anything he'd much rather be at the competition right now, even if he won't admit that to me, even on pain of death.

You and me both, dude.

I mean, really.

We've been here only maybe twenty minutes, but it's already starting to feel like it's been twenty-*five* minutes too long. The air is thick with Mom's signature scent, J-Lo's Glow, and I swear to God it's starting to give me hives. The main atrium of the library actually isn't that small—it's a wide, vaulted space with amazing moldings and a polished but rustic wide-planked floor—but I'm still feeling like I've been squished into an overcrowded elevator and someone hit the Emergency button. It's like there's not enough oxygen in the room for both Mom and me to be breathing at the same time. And Mom, as usual, is working overtime, pulling way more than her own allotment into those heaving lungs.

"*Ay, Dios mío!*" she exclaims now, waving a meticulously (and artificially) bronzed arm toward one of her framed prints. It's the one of Ricky Ricardo dressed up for Halloween. "You would not believe how long it took me to get this *perfecto* shot." Whoever it is she's talking to—a doughy woman I don't recognize—nods along solemnly, as though in awe of Mom's great ability to stay on task and capture the dog in all of his costumed glory.

Or maybe she's just hypnotized by Mom's earrings.

"Are those . . . *peacock feathers*?" Duncan asks, noting the earrings at that very moment.

(Of course, there are people in *China* who can probably see the earrings right now, too. Straight through the core of the earth and everything. They are *that* intense.)

"They sure as heck are." Bright, turquoise-and-black, shoulder-grazing peacock feathers. I know she chose them specifically for how they offset her white satin halter jumpsuit.

Her *white satin halter jumpsuit,* people. In *Alaska.*

I just hope the population of China is ready for her.

Duncan sighs. "Sometimes your mother is made of awesome."

Oh, Dunc. I glare at him. "Wanna trade?"

He doesn't dignify me with an answer, but instead shimmies over to a side table where some sad-looking snacks are hanging out, potato chips and plastic bowls of hummus posing as real, grown-up party food, but failing miserably.

(Side note: plastic bowls = not-grown-up. Sorry, but it's the truth.)

"Your mom seems happy with the turnout," Duncan comments, stuffing a hummus-laden potato chip (oh, yak) into his mouth.

"I think she's just happy to have an excuse to wear those shoes." They're Lacroix violet-snakeskin wedges. She must have swapped her *h*'Uggs at the door.

"Yeah, well. Can you blame her?"

I can and I do. I can and I do, Duncan dear.

We mill, and drink sparkling water—which is just like

regular water, except sneeze-inducing, which is less fun than it might sound. I inhale as tentatively as I can manage to avoid sneezing all over my "date," and pick at the potato chips. It's easy to resist them since they're the fancy kind that are made of random and bizarre organic vegetables. Blech. Not worth it.

A few more swallows of hummus, and we've run out of ways to amuse ourselves. I'm still not moved by the chips situation. I decide, "Let's find my dad."

Duncan raises an eyebrow. "Nothing against your dad, but there's gotta be someone here who's more exciting than he is."

I make a face. "No, dummy. He's going to make a toast. He said we could leave once the toast was done. Ergo . . ." I make a rolling gesture with my hand that indicates where said toast could lead us.

Duncan's face lights up as he connects the dots. "Ergo, the sooner we get this clinkity-clank under way, the sooner we can *vamanoose*."

"Yes. Except don't say 'clinkity-clank.' And that's not exactly real Spanish, you know."

Duncan goes, "What's your point?"

And I realize that I don't have one.

■▪▮▮

Down the hallway and past the hubbub, we find an office that's been set up as a dumping ground for Mom. It's small and cluttered, but she has still managed to take it over with an oversized tote bag worthy of an Olsen twin and roomy enough to cart around half of the library's shelves.

Or, you know, six extra Juicy hoodies in various colors. Just in case of emergency.

(What *really* would constitute a "Juicy emergency"? Seriously, people. Let's talk about this. I'm looking for your input.)

Duncan puts his hands on his hips and scans the cramped space. "I'm gonna go out on a limb and say that I don't think your dad is in here. Unless he's picked up some contortionist skills of late, and is chillin', like, in one of those file cabinets or something."

"Yeah, probably not." But there is this strange noise, like a hiss or a hum, coming from underneath the round table that sits in the middle of the room. "Do you hear that?" I cock my head to one side.

"What?"

"Shh!" I definitely can't hear it when Duncan is talking, but for sure there's some kind of buzz. Coming from *somewhere*. I just can't tell . . .

I crouch down. "Do you think it's the heater?"

We hear a sharp, yelping bark.

"I do not think that was the heater," Duncan says. "I emphatically do not think so."

Ricky Ricardo bounds out from under the table and straight at me, wiggling like a bowl of Jell-O but bounding forward with surprisingly fierce intent.

"Hey, boy," I say, carefully extracting his tiny claws from my cardigan and easing him down onto the ground. "What are you doing here? Since when does Mom let you out of her sight? And on an *especial* occasion." *Especially* given that I can now see she's affixed a ginormous peacock feather to his silver glitter collar. Festive.

"Your mom's got bigger *tortillas* to fry today," Duncan says, joining me on his knees on the floor. "But what did he have in his mouth? I think that's what was making the buzzing sound." He fully scoots himself underneath the table, shoves a few different objects around. "Oh—is this your mother's . . ."

His voice trails off. No buzz, no chatter, just the steady rasp of Ricky's panting.

Now I'm curious.

"Is *what* my mother's?" I crawl forward, wishing I could clear the tabletop as easily as Duncan did. I glance over, stare at the object he holds in his hands.

It's a BlackBerry. Mom's.

And Duncan's face is aflame.

I lean in, lightning quick, and snatch the 'Berry from him.

"Ricky was using this as a chew toy?" I marvel. "She is *so* going to love that." With Duncan's abashed expression still unwavering, I scan the screen. This had better be good. I start to process actual strings of words: *miss you . . . so cute when you . . . Beautiful . . .*

I cackle. "My *dad* has been sending Mom flirty e-mails? That's priceless." I pause mid–knee slap. "Priceless and *gross*. Having seen it will probably lead to at least two years of therapy for me in later life. I mean, parentals aren't supposed to do the flirty-flirt, right? Because of the age factor? And the *ick* factor?"

I giggle again, but Duncan's not laughing with me. In fact, he looks like he has swallowed some *ick* himself.

"What's your damage, dude? Is there a sexy picture attached that you happened to stumble upon? Wait—no, don't tell me." I try to keep my tone playful, despite the gnawing feeling in my stomach that we took a sharp left turn from *playful* a few miles back there, somewhere.

When Duncan *still* stays rigid, my body goes slack. Whatever he saw, it obviously can't be joked away.

That can't be good.

He finally meets my gaze, clearly unwilling. Uneager. "Check the signature of the e-mail, Aggie," he says, quieter than I think I've ever heard him speak. He looks sickened. "Read it."

So I do.

And.

Oh, barf.

Speaking of therapy, and *ick*, and all things disturbing. *Speaking* of sickening.

My mother.

Has been exchanging love letters.

With *Christopher. Young.* As in Mr. Young. *Senior.*

Though the basic facts of biology prevent me from being able to see my own expression, I'd bet money that it mirrors Duncan's. Mirrors it, and amplifies it by 16,082 percent.

When the BlackBerry slips from my fingers and hits the ground, I allow myself a moment to hope that I've actually broken it. That I've somehow managed to crack this moment in half, to shatter the hideous news that has just smashed my own life into tiny little jagged pieces.

But wouldn't you know?

No such luck.

Qué lástima, Agacita. Indeed.

CHAPTER 21

"Aggie!"

Duncan calls after me, his voice echoing against the walls of the library hallway. But I don't slow.

"Come on, Aggie, where are you going? What are you doing?" His footsteps are heavy and almost in sync with my own.

He needn't worry. I'm not going to, like, make a whole big scene or anything. Not here, heaven forbid, in front of Mom's adoring public. *God*, no. *Obviously.*

I mean, despite the fact that she clearly doesn't have one iota of respect for me, for my father, for our *family*—calling Mom out right here in the middle of everything would never be my style.

We all *know* how I feel about being the center of attention, right?

What I *don't* know: which of us, then, makes me sicker right now—my mother, or myself?

Survey says: it's a total draw. A washout. So.

Well. Maybe Making a Whole Dramatic Thing isn't me, but if I've learned one thing since arriving in Alaska, it's: How to Express Myself.

Boy, howdy.

I stomp right up to my mother, feeling my features screw in anger and hurt. Her heavily penciled eyebrows knit in confusion as she sees me approach. "*Qué pasa?*" she asks, her tone overly bright, clearly hoping that my expression is just a figment of her über-active imagination.

Not a chance, Mamacita.

I face off in front of her, jaw set, breathing heavily.

I say, "I think you may have dropped this."

I slap the BlackBerry—the most incriminating, gag-inducing message open and shining out like a beacon of betrayal—down into her waiting palm.

And then I turn and run.

.ıll

When Duncan finds me, I am hiding in the restroom at the diner.

He cracks open the door to the ladies' room and nods when he sees me, leaning dejectedly against the basin of the sink.

"Loitering in public bathrooms," he says, making a face.

"Bad news. No good can come of this."

I have to laugh at that. "There couldn't be anything worse than what we've already, uh, learned," I insist. "Besides, I'm hiding. Not loitering. They are very different activities."

"Good job," he says. "Found you. Tag, you're it." He motions like he's tapping me on the shoulder.

"Maybe if some people didn't flagrantly disregard the same-sex regulations pertaining to public bathrooms . . ."

"Cady told me you were in here alone. She gave me the go-ahead."

Well, then. "Okay."

Except, nothing is okay.

After a moment, Duncan goes, "I know," as though I've said something else, even though I haven't. He crosses the room and pulls me away from the sink. Then he pats my shoulder for real.

It helps, a little.

"Sweetie," he says, "we *so* have better places we could be right now."

.•Il

Duncan tells me there's still time to hit the ski competition, but the thought of seeing Tobin sends my stomach into free fall. It's one thing to know that he's taken, but it's another level of *eek* entirely to think that our parents have gotten flirtier than he and I have. Instead, Dunc drives me back to my house, and we investigate the latest of my cell phone's shenanigans, purely out of curiosity. It's an exercise in futility, though; I'm not sure what, exactly, would feel like the right thing to do, right at this very moment in time, but miniature golf isn't it. That much, I know.

In the end, I convince Duncan that I'm stable enough to be left alone, and once he's driven off, I spend a few mindless hours skimming the Internet for celebrity scandals, preferring that ridiculosity to the grotesque telenovela-style circus that my own life has suddenly become. If I'd thought that Tobin was off-limits before, he has since graduated to Teflon levels. Toxic.

El sueño imposible. The impossible dream.

Saying it in a foreign language doesn't pretty up the truth at all. Not one eensy-weensy, teeny-tiny bit.

Cómo se dice "hopeless" *en Español,* anyway?

CHAPTER 22

I fall asleep before Mom and

Dad come back from the show. Which is one way of avoiding unpleasant topics. My cell phone would be disappointed in me, sure, but at this very moment, I simply can't be bothered.

Duncan IM's me Sunday morning, asks if I want to do brunch with him and some people from the ski team. I resist the urge to do the whole "I told you so," thing re: his ski-bunny stalkee, but when I ask who else will be tagging along, briefly contemplating reembracing personal hygiene and wondering when was the last time I washed my hair, he IM's Tobin *and* Riley. And then I lose my appetite all over again. Even though Tobin and Riley are the only couple in any of this mess who, in theory, aren't gag-reflex inducing.

I have no plans to emerge from the cocoon that I've woven out of my various throw blankets. (For once, I'm grateful for the excess of bedding, but I refuse to give Mom any credit for her foresight. Considering she was the one who created the crisis scenario to begin with, and all.) I figure I'll have to go back to school on Monday morning, but if Tobin—and Riley—will be there, then at least my mom *won't*. I'm trying to calculate the possibility of making it to, say, my own college graduation without breaking the vow of Mom silence I've committed to, when the door to my bedroom bursts open, and there she is, standing before me, in all of her tracksuited . . .

Well, it's not *glory*. Not exactly. In fact, by Mom's usual standards, I have to admit, she looks pretty subdued. She's wearing navy, which is as close as she gets to basic black, and her face is scrubbed clean and free of makeup. Her hair is pulled back in a low ponytail and—are her nails really *bare*? I do a double take. Yup: polish-free. And clipped down. *Clipped down.*

And Ricky Ricardo is nowhere in sight. Curiouser and curiouser.

Well, at least I know she's taking this situation seriously.

I turn toward her warily, not speaking but not overtly telling—or even asking—her to leave, either. It's pretty clear she has something important to say.

She nods at me, assessing my state, and makes her way into the room, settling tentatively at the edge of my bed. I pull my knees up to my chest underneath the covers and scoot back until I'm pressed against the wall, swaddled tightly.

"I'm sorry." Her voice cracks, and she glances down at the floor.

It's a good start.

I don't breathe, don't move, don't even blink. I want to know what comes next, but still don't trust my own vocal cords. It's okay; Mom has more that she's prepared. Even though I can tell from the lines on her forehead that the words she's speaking are causing her actual, physical pain.

"I was wrong."

"Correct." Ah—*there's* my voice. A little wobblier than I would like, but still. Functioning. Which is huge.

"I should never have been *h'exchanging* those messages with Tobin's *padre*."

News from the Department of Duh, *folks.*

"He's *my friend's father!*" I explode, bringing my hands down flat against the top of my mattress, sending us both bouncing lightly in place. "And he's married. Like *you* are."

"Nothing really happened. *Nada.* I promise you this. *Pero*, that doesn't make the messages and the . . . feelings behind them right."

"You have *feelings* for Mr. Young?" There isn't enough bedding in the world to sufficiently buffer me from the impact of this moment. I need, like, a motorcycle helmet. Or a plastic bubble. Or a moat.

Yeah. A moat. A moat would be nice. Where does a

regular gal like myself find a good, old-fashioned protective moat these days?

"*Agacita.*"

"You don't get to call me that right now," I warn her. Frankly, she's lucky I'm even pretending to hear her out.

"Aggie," she concedes. "I'm human. *Mira,* I'm telling you, I know it was wrong, all of it—but I'm human. I had feelings."

"*Had.*"

"I thought your father and I, we had a good marriage. But I was lonely here. The *fotografías,* they weren't enough. And *para mí* I learned that I was jealous that your father's star was rising while mine was . . . fading." She folds her hands in her lap, looking uncharacteristically chastened. Can it be that she's really been picking at her cuticles? Yowza.

Well. I am not even one minuscule fraction less angry at her than I was before. But I *do* kind of feel sorry for her. *Kind* of.

I mean, like, not *that* much. But still.

But.

Still.

She must see the "still" slide down my face, because she goes on. "I went to the dogsled place. For the tour. But Tobin wasn't there—he was with you, with the *e*-ski practice."

Yeah, nice try, Mom. There's no way this is *at all* my

fault. Sorry, but survey says: FAIL. Try again later.

"So Mr. Young, he gave me the tour, and we . . . how do you say . . . clicked. He is funny. And sweet."

Like father, like son, I think miserably.

"And I went to visit him a few more times during the *semana,* and we starting talking on the *telefono.* And then there were . . . the text messages."

My expression hardens, darkening like a thundercloud. I can't hear about the text messages. It's too, too many levels of *ick.*

She leans forward and reaches for my hand. "What I did was wrong, Aggie, but I promise you, *nothing* happened."

And really, I get what she means, and you know, I'm glad to hear that she never got to first base with Tobin's father, really, I am, but still, this is not nearly as comforting as she obviously means for it to be.

"Mom, you agreed to come to Alaska!" I sputter. "Your star wasn't fading—that was a choice you made!" Okay, so maybe it was a hard choice, a sucky choice, sure—part of why I spent so many years avoiding the difficult task of actively choosing. I appreciate that choices are often not so easy-peasy. But she's a grown-up! Difficult tasks are, I'm sorry to say, her responsibility.

"*Aggie.*" She speaks very slowly, clearly, like she means for me really to hear what she is saying, now. The syllables roll off her tongue with deliberate focus, attention.

She leans in. "The network let me go. That was why it was so 'easy' for me to agree to come to Alaska with your father. You think I didn't consider staying behind with you? Maybe arranging for weekend *vacaciones*?" She swallows, hard. "But they don't want me on the show anymore. They say I am too old to play the part of Milagros. They're bringing in a younger girl to take over the role."

I gasp, sitting up very straight now and pushing down some of my covers. This is something I did not, could not have seen coming.

We've seen the same thing happen with other actresses on plenty of soaps, Mom and I, but I can say with confidence that, for my part, it never occurred to me that something like this would ever happen to my mother. She's been playing the part of Milagros forever—ages, literally. Since I've been old enough to remember. The part was created specially for her. It never occurred to any of us that it could ever be taken away from her.

I know actress years are like dog years, and I know that soaps have a high turnover, but for some reason, I always just took it for granted that rules didn't apply when it came to my own mother.

I'm an idiot. Clearly.

And *Mom* . . .

Poor Mom.

I think back to all of the times that she's prodded me, prompted me to take better care of myself, to exercise more, to eat well, to slap some lip gloss on once in a while, or to consider, however briefly, a tinted moisturizer or a straightening iron. I think about how simple, how one-sided it was of me to assume that she was being vain, being shallow, thinking of *me* only as yet another accessory, an extension of her own overly adorned self.

And I realize: every interaction I've ever had with my mother about my own body, my style, my looks, has been informed by *her* experience of spending her entire adult life worrying that her looks were only her commodity. Were her *only* commodity.

Only finally, then, to be proven right.

It's almost enough to make me *glad* I've clung so fervently to my no-frills lifestyle.

Almost.

Except I promised my cell phone I'd stop lying to myself.

I promised my cell phone: no more secrets.

And my cell phone knows that buried beneath all of that moody blah-blah; the gray, tenty sweaters and drawstring waistbands—underneath those things was some big-time, plus-sized, XXL jealousy on my part. Jealous of my mom: her slammin' bod, her self-control, her confidence.

And—okay, yeah, you got me—her peacock earrings.

I mean: *made of awesome,* people. Can you even?

Peacock. *Earrings.*

All at once, I burst into tears.

Not soft, gentle feminine tears, like the ones that roll slowly down your face, one at a time, leaving only a slim trail of sadness across a perfect expanse of porcelain cheek. No, that would be soap-opera crying. *Weeping,* if you will. Weeping is gentle and operatic.

My tears are nothing like soap-opera crying.

I sob—heaving, gasping, and gulping at air like a drowning victim, hiccupping and sniffling and rubbing the heel of my palm against my red, runny nose.

If Tobin could see me now. It's not my finest moment. And I can't even pinpoint exactly what it is, precisely, that I'm crying *about*—I mean, pick a number, right?—but it sort of doesn't matter. It feels good to let go.

And then Mom shuffles closer to me and wraps her arms more tightly around me than any chenille throw could be tucked.

And then, it even feels good—kind of—to feel bad.

We sit that way for a bit, me bawling, and snotting, and generally being lame, and Mom patting me, and rocking me, and generally being awesome, until my big, noisy, boo-hoo crybaby thing finally dies down to the point where it's only a residual stray whimper here and there. It feels like—I don't know, like maybe that moment when the ice shelf first cracks, and the fracture spreads outward, along the horizon. And then the glacier snaps, detaches, breaks off from the solid formation of shelf. And begins, finally, to wander away.

I don't know. Maybe it's like that.

And then.

Mom reaches up, and with her neat, filed-down, so-un-Mom-like fingertips, smooths my hair back off of my forehead, where she plants a dry, warm, un-glossy Mom kiss.

She says, "Come back to Miami with me, *Agacita*."

If there's one thing that I've learned from my wayward cell phone, it's that sunrise is a good time for all manner of head clearing. So on Monday morning, I dust off my lined track pants and Thinsulated boots and head off to the lookout point on the edge of town.

Maybe six weeks ago, it would have been disconcerting to be poised, hands on hips, breathing clouds of vapor into the slurry mix of watery snow flurries as the sun paints the horizon in bold, vibrant swatches of gold and red. Especially given as how it's ten in the morning (thank you, post-Thanksgiving, pre-announced study hall). But today, it only feels natural to choose this as the location at which to meditate over Mom's offer.

She's going back to Miami. Her agent called with a new job, the role of a scandalized starter wife plotting an elaborate revenge scheme against her ex and his new mistress; she's to appear in a minimum of ten episodes of *El*

Mundo Fantastico. It's a far cry from the manipulative diva cougars she's been playing of late, natch, but it's work. And say what you will about Spanish-language soaps, it's what she knows, what she's good at.

What do *I* know?

I know that there *are* a few things, in point of fact, that I'm good at. That there is, actually, an adventurous streak, buried not quite as deeply within as I might have once thought. That I don't ever need to recover my cell phone, and that, frankly, I can cancel the account and move on to actually challenging *myself* to live out loud.

But I still don't know whether or not I'm going to go with her.

She and Dad talked things through, and Dad put on his Understanding Ears. I don't think he was any more pleased than I was to hear about Mom's "sexting scandal," but they are definitely staying together. This whole Alaskan adventure was never meant to be a permanent thing; Dad's contract is up come June, so it's only a matter of whether or not I want to go back now, or stick it out until the end of the year. And the truth is, though I never thought in a zillion gajillion years that I would be saying this:

I'm torn.

"Aggie?"

I flinch, startled. I turn to find Tobin standing behind me, curiosity etched across his face. He's holding out a steaming Styrofoam to-go cup.

"What are you doing here?" My heart begins to pound loudly in my rib cage, and it's not from the physical exertion, I promise you that.

"When you weren't in study hall, I figured I might find you here. I know you like to go walking in the mornings. I've seen you in town, you know."

"Oh, right." At the diner. But. "I didn't think you . . . uh, remembered that. Thought about that."

He tilts his head at me. "Thought about you?"

I blush. "Yeah. I guess I didn't think . . . that."

"I was bummed you couldn't come to the ski competition. I mean, I know you had your mom's thing."

"Right." Wait. "What?"

Tobin shrugs, looking slightly embarrassed. "My dad told me. About everything. Since I guess your mom spoke to him about how you found the BlackBerry." He pauses, takes a breath. "But it looks like it was nothing."

I say, "My mom is going back to Miami."

"Yeah, I heard about that. And that you might go with her."

"I don't know."

"Well." His face burns a bright tomato color. "I hope you don't." He thrusts the to-go cup at me. "I brought you hot chocolate."

Um, *huh?*

The boy. *Brought me hot chocolate.*

Hold the phones, people. This is starting to get *muy interesante.*

I reach out, take the cup, allowing our fingertips to brush. Despite the fact that our hands are covered in thick gloves, the contact still gives me shivers. I take a sip, allowing the milky liquid to slide languidly down my throat.

Then I square my shoulders to be brave, to make the hard, sucky choice. "My mom, and your dad—" That's about as close as I can get to saying the actual words.

"No, no," Tobin interrupts. "I mean, I know. So it's weird. But still, maybe."

Maybe. I like the sound of that. *Maybe.*

Except, there's still the little matter of, "Riley?" I can barely bring myself to squeak out the two syllables.

Tobin sighs heavily. "Yeah, that was kind of a mess."

Was kind of a mess. Interesting use of the past tense. Feel free to go on, Toby . . .

"I mean, you know that she and I used to date. And I guess she wanted to start things back up again."

I guess.

"I tried, you know . . ." He looks sheepish. "It was stupid. That relationship was over a long time ago. But I guess I got stuck in some kind of a rut. Like, a holding pattern. Where it was easier to go along with things than it would have been to make, like, a real decision." He kicks at the snow, sending little sprays out in an arc. "Dumb."

"It happens," I say, because: it happens. I should know. Once upon a time, inertia was my best friend.

Things are different for me, now.

"What do you think?" Tobin asks, like he's waiting for an answer to a question he hasn't asked. A question I've been waiting six weeks to hear.

What do I think? I think that I have No. Effing. Idea. *What* to think.

I go, "Um."

Brilliant, Ag. For serious.

"I told Riley . . . I told her I couldn't be with her. Because . . . well, because I have feelings for someone else."

I nod, slightly numb, despite the hot chocolate. Is this really happening? Is Tobin *really* saying what I think he's saying?

Squee-age. *Major* squee-age.

"She won't be mad," he assures me. "She's pretty mature and stuff."

Of course she is. Goes hand in hand with her divine perfection. Gag.

"But you might want to stay out of Tegan's way for a while. She can be a little overprotective of her friends."

I giggle.

Once upon a time, I might have cared what Tegan thought of me. But things are different now.

Once upon a time, inertia was my best friend.

Things are different for me, now.

So the question is still, What do I think?

Believe it or not, I know.

I *do* know what I think, after all. I think, my cell phone has always had just the right idea. And that there's no time like the present. And:

"I want to go on a wildlife tour. With you, I mean. If you're interested. Like, maybe on one of your dad's dogsleds. Or, you know, Bob's Original. It comes highly recommended." By, um, an inanimate object, but that's hardly the point here. My cell phone is an expert on living large.

Tobin goes, "Okay. Sounds good."

And I think, it sounds so much more than *good,* that good is just a baby microdot on the edge of the horizon, totally blurred by the streaks of sunlight dancing against the late-morning sky.

I do one of those random active choicey things, one of those things Miami-Aggie would have never ever thought to attempt:

I fling my arms around Tobin.

(Side note: I drop my hot chocolate in the snow in the process, but OH. EM. GEE. *Who cares?*)

And I kiss him squarely on the lips.

It's closemouthed, and quick, but still firm and soft and dazzling enough to buckle my knees ever so slightly. He feels the shake in my legs, kisses back, wraps his fingers around my arms to steady me. Even though at this exact very moment in time, unsteady feels totally and completely just right.

We pull apart, and he grins at me, his warmth washing over me, better than hot chocolate, or sunshine, or even that pounding in the space behind your ears.

He whispers, "You look so cute in that huge parka."

And I go, "I know." Because I do.

Although.

I'm thinking it might be time to pick up another coat. Something shiny and new. Something sunny and bright. Not orange, because, you know: citrus fruit. But still. Maybe even—*gasp*—something in a rich, brilliant red.

I have to say, I think my cell phone would approve.

Acknowledgments

My most sincere gratitude goes to Jodi Reamer, for knowing the winning pitch when she heard it, and to Kristin Gilson, for shaping that pitch into a full story, in its best possible incarnation (and for taking the editorial additions of a crazed—but well-dressed—Chihuahua and a retired telenovela star in stride). To Kathi Appelt and Sharon Darrow, for early reads and enthusiasm. To Kristen Pettit, for a premise and a spark. To Judy Goldschmidt and Lynn Weingarten, for the catharsis of collective insanity. To Nova Ren Suma, for staggering talent and for inspiring the type of professional jealousy that pushes me to work harder. To Katharine Sise, for good karma.

To my family, which has multiplied over recent years: Mom, Dad, David, Lily, Liz, Len, Fleur, and Josh.

And to Noah, who has always been the prize awaiting me at the end of my personal scavenger hunt. If my cell phone had GPS, babe (or, rather, if I knew how to use it), I am certain it would lead me to you.